CHRISTMAS
IN MY HEART

9

Home for Christmas

There is an empty chair in the parlor
An empty bed in the guestroom
There is an empty plate on the table
An empty place in the heart.

Still can be heard the sound
Of childish laughter
Still the unmistakable muffled sound
Of childish tears.

There was love in this house
Love in every pore
And God was in this house
Morning, noon, and night.

The house is quiet now
The children grown and far away
The letters, oh the letters are so few
And the telephone's so still.

But listen, Father, could that be a car in the
    driveway?
Voices, such familiar voices
The children! Oh Mother!
The children—all the children—have come home.

Joseph Leininger Wheeler

FOCUS ON THE FAMILY®

CHRISTMAS IN MY HEART

A TREASURY OF TIMELESS
CHRISTMAS STORIES

9

compiled and edited by
JOE L. WHEELER

TYNDALE HOUSE PUBLISHERS, INC., WHEATON, ILLINOIS

Visit Tyndale's exciting Web site at www.tyndale.com

Focus on the Family is a registered trademark of Focus on the Family, Colorado Springs, Colorado.

Christmas in My Heart is a registered trademark of Joe L. Wheeler and may not be used by anyone else in any form.

Author photo by Joel Springer © 2000. All rights reserved.

Woodcut illustrations are from the library of Joe L. Wheeler.

Designed by Jenny Destree.

Published in association with the literary agency of Alive Communications, Inc., 7680 Goddard St., Suite 200, Colorado Springs, Colorado 80920.

Scripture quotations are taken from the *Holy Bible,* King James Version.

Library of Congress Cataloging in Publication Data

Christmas in my heart/ [compiled by] Joe L.Wheeler.
   p. cm.
   ISBN 0-8423-5189-2 (9)
   1. Christmas stories, American.   I. Wheeler, Joe L., date
PS648.C45C447   1992
813'.010833—dc20

CIP

Printed in the United States of America

06   05   04   03   02   01   00
7   6   5   4   3   2   1

DEDICATION

Long ago, as far back as *Christmas in My Heart 1*, she
read the stories, fell in love with them, and encouraged
me to hold the course. Through the years her continued
encouragement has remained a constant. Her voice
brightens the darkest day, because of the joy bells in it.

Gracious, thoughtful, kind, appreciative, dependable,
she is the kind of a friend who warms the soul, who
comes into the heart—and stays there.

It gives me great pleasure to dedicate
Christmas in My Heart 9 to

DIANE PASSNO
of
Focus on the Family.

CONTENTS

ACKNOWLEDGMENTS

"Home for Christmas," (a poem) by Joseph Leininger Wheeler. Copyright © 2000. Printed by permission of the author.

"Home for Christmas," by Joseph Leininger Wheeler. Copyright © 2000. Printed by permission of the author.

"Waiting . . . Waiting for Christmas," by Elizabeth King English. Reprinted by permission from *Guideposts,* December, 1983. Copyright © 1983 by *Guideposts,* Carmel, NY 19512.

"His Guiding Star," by Mary Agnes Jackman. Published in *Nor-West Farmer,* Winnipeg, December 5, 1929. If anyone can provide knowledge of first publication source and current ownership of the rights to this old story, please relay this information to Joe Wheeler in care of Tyndale House Publishers, P.O. Box 80, Wheaton, IL 60189.

"Holly at the Door," by Agnes Sligh Turnbull. Published in *McCall's,* December, 1926. If anyone can provide knowledge of first publication source and current ownership of the rights to this old story, please relay this information to Joe Wheeler in care of Tyndale House Publishers.

"Christmas Is for Kids," by Nancy N. Rue. Published in *Brio,* December, 1994. Reprinted by permission of the author.

"The Bells Didn't Ring," by Isabel T. Dingman. Published in *Nor-West Farmer,* Winnipeg, December 5, 1929. If anyone can provide knowledge of first publication source and current ownership of the rights to this old story, please relay this information to Joe Wheeler in care of Tyndale House Publishers.

"A Rose in Winter," by Jodi Detrick. Copyright © 1996. Reprinted by permission of the author.

"An Ill Wind," by Frederick William Roe. Published in *The Youth's Companion,* January 2, 1919.

"Carla's Christmas Gift," by Judith Wade. Published in *What to Do,* December 20, 1942. Text reprinted by permission of David C. Cook Publishing, Colorado Springs, CO.

"Bulger's Friends," by O. Henry. Published in *The Youth's Companion,* December 26, 1901.

"The Town That Gave Us Joy," by Marian Jeppson Walker. Published in *Family Circle*, December 16, 1997. Reprinted by permission of the author.

"The Forgotten Friend," by Grace Livingston Hill. Included in Hill's *Miss Lavinia's Call and Other Stories* (Philadelphia and New York: J. B. Lippincott Company, 1949). Reprinted by permission of R. L. Munce Publishing, Inc.

"How an Unborn Baby Saved Its Mother's Life," by Joseph A. MacDougall, as told to Douglas How. Published in *The Telegraph Journal*, St. John, New Brunswick, December 22, 1984. Reprinted by permission of *The Telegraph Journal* and Douglas How.

"A Christmas Experience," author unknown. If anyone can provide knowledge of the authorship, origin, and first publication source of this story, please relay this information to Joe Wheeler in care of Tyndale House Publishers.

"Like a Candle in the Window," by Margaret E. Sangster, Jr. If anyone can provide knowledge of the first publication source of this old story, please relay this information to Joe Wheeler in care of Tyndale House Publishers.

"City of Dreams," by Joseph Leininger Wheeler. Copyright © 1999. Printed by permission of the author.

Joseph Leininger Wheeler

INTRODUCTION: HOME FOR CHRISTMAS

"Home for Christmas"—are there sweeter words in the English language? After all, taken singly, "home" and "Christmas" are two of the most loaded-with-sentiment words we know. Together, their freight is almost mind-boggling.

We all conceptualize in concrete terms. Consequently, when we think of going home, we visualize it first as a part of the country; next as a town or place; then as a farm, ranch, or piece of ground; and finally as a building. It is because of this sequential perception of home that the first wave of homecoming joy washes over us when we enter the region of home: Whatever it be, mountains, rolling hills, plains, desert, or seacoast, the effect is the same.

Since I was born only a few miles from the coast of California, when driving west I sense I'm nearing home once the car crests the Sierra Nevadas and starts down toward the San Joaquin Valley. But when my senses tell me the ocean is near—even before I can see it—a much bigger wave of joy floods me and, oh, that first vision of the Pacific! It almost stops my heart. It is the ocean that represents "home" to me, since there is no ancestral home still in family hands and I cannot bear to seek out my grandparents' Napa Valley Shangri-la high on Howell Mountain. I fear what I'd find after the long years (perhaps it is now demolished completely), and I'd rather dream that it still exists as I once knew and loved it. But having been born in the mountains, as I was in a sense in the Napa Valley region, I feel that they are home, too. Of course, for those born on the Great Plains, the mountains might be claustrophobic, and to those born and raised on the desert, no other terrain can ever be as beautiful as the sunburned and windswept sage.

Some blessed few are fortunate enough to be born and to do their growing up in one locale, one house, and be able to return to it late in life, finding it intact and still in the family. But few of us are that lucky. Some months ago, my sister Marjorie and I took my mother to Chico, California, where Mom had lived for a time in her earliest childhood. We found the right street easily enough, but a number of the landmarks my mother remembered were no longer there. Finally we narrowed our search down to a two-block area, then one. Then we found it—the home where Mother had lived! Fortunately, Chico has preserved the street as a historic district. We went in and found out her former home is a doctor's office now, but amazingly the lovely old place, surrounded by towering trees, had seen very little remodeling in eighty years. Mother showed us the bedroom that had been hers and the window through which she viewed her childhood world. To Marjorie and me that window represented a part of our mother we had never known. And, in truth, to recapture a part of our parents is to recapture a part of ourselves as well.

Being the child of teachers, a minister father, missionary parents, I have no one childhood place to consider home. That's why the homes of my paternal and maternal grandparents meant so much to me, for no matter where my parents moved, those two houses remained constants we could depend on. Without such symbols of stability, children feel lost. Readers may remember my paternal grandparents' Napa Valley home from my story, "Legacy," in *Christmas in My Heart 8*. But I had another home to return to as well: a great rambling two-story house in Arcata, California, belonging to Grandma and Grandpa Leininger. I lived with them my eighth-grade year, and that year, one of the most happy and loved periods of my lifetime, is woven into the very fiber of my being.

In those far-off days before so much logging had taken place, Arcata was one of the foggiest places on the planet, very conducive to the acres of fuchsia, asters, and other flowers that Grandpa grew for his florist business. Behind the house (readers may remember it in my Christmas story, "The Third Rose," in *Christmas in My Heart 3* and in *Great Stories Remembered II*) was a towering redwood forest that seemed to stretch away forever to my childish eyes. It was complete with trilliums, ferns, and a magical lake that I considered my own possession. Across Highway 101 we could hear the sounds of the lumber mill night and day. At night, I'd look out my attic window at the ghostly headlights—heading I knew not where on the highway—and I'd dream of the people inside and wonder about their destinations.

HOME IS WHERE LOVE IS

Since my parents moved so often, when I conceptualize "home" in my mind I telescope a number of houses in a number of countries, each of which was home for a time. What counted was my parents' love for each other: *that* was the real essence of home to us. As long as that remained constant, moving from one set of four walls to another was merely another adventure. When a move had been completed and the furniture and possessions had been reassembled in the old way, we children were just as much at home as before the move took place.

Which brings us to the sad reality of a divorce-ridden society. In my lifetime of research, reading, and dealing with students of all ages, I have become convinced beyond a shadow of a doubt that a child *never* fully recovers from separation or divorce. I have heard many adult children of divorce tell their life stories, and over and over again, whether the interval is six months or sixty years, the result is the same: When they come to that period of separation, they slow their telling or reading, they begin to choke up, tears begin to flow, and often the story grinds to a complete halt. The group is forced to leave for a while, reassemble, and hope the man or woman will find it possible to continue.

The act of desertion creates a chasm in the child's psyche, a gulf that separates the world that was from the world that comes after. *Never* does that chasm close, even when the parents remarry. The terrible damage to the child's sense of selfhood, self-worth, and belonging cannot be undone, no matter how many years may pass.

Children of divorce have seen something tragic happen to the protective walls of home, that fortress each of us needs to retreat into during the struggles of life. So it is that when a child of separation or divorce thinks of "home" at Christmastime, it will be in a different way than children of an undivided family. Home to the child of divorce may very well be a fragmentation between four or more sets of step-relationships: thus, no one of them is perceived holistically. But this does not mean that a home with a stepparent may not be seen as the closest and dearest home that child could imagine, for some blessed stepparents bring to that later home all the qualities that were missing in the first.

THE REWARDS OF GOING HOME
Having said all this, when the subject comes up as to whether or not to go home for Christmas, other variables come into play, chief of which is this question: Are the rewards of going home worth the expenditure of effort and money? If bickering is likely, the answer is probably no. If all anyone does there is watch TV, that could be done just as easily and much more inexpensively by staying put. No, those who will joyfully invest

effort, time, and money in going home for Christmas do so because going there is likely to be such joy—camaraderie, expressed love, family traditions, music, church, games, food, laughter, reading of stories, nonstop talk, adventuring out on side trips en masse or in smaller groups, watching favorite Christmas movies or videos—that it would be unthinkable not to be part of it.

Going home also demonstrates to each of us a great truth: We are all getting older—the children become teenagers, the teenagers become young adults, the young adults become young marrieds, the young marrieds become parents, the parents become middle-aged, the middle-aged become senior citizens, and the senior citizens lose their mental and physical edge and then are taken from the holiday festivities by death. Thus, we do indeed measure our lives by our Christmases. Bitter though it is to see those we love weakening under the battering of the years, it does make us love and cherish them the more, recognizing that the time may not be far off when we will no longer have that privilege. Furthermore, when that sad day *does* come at last, we will still have all the wondrous memories to replay each Christmas—"Remember the time when"—and it is as though that dearly beloved person is part of the circle still.

THE RETURN TO VALUES AND TRADITIONS

Interestingly enough, today even the children of divorce are seeking a stability and sense of bedrock they never knew. Traditions are coming back again, as are other "old-fashioned" values such as integrity, decency, loyalty, faithfulness, kindness, empathy, generosity, altruism, dependability, and selflessness. In the words of the musical *Carousel,* we as a society had "gone about as far as we could go" in the opposite direction of these qualities. Now, across the nation, a new emphasis is developing on values, family, and traditions that enrich life. Not surprisingly, there is renewed interest in making holidays such as Christmas not only more enjoyable but also more meaningful.

But going home for Christmas presupposes the existence of other things. These are (1) the stability that comes with God-sanctified marriage as opposed to live-in relationships, (2) children—how true it is that none of us really grows up and becomes truly unselfish until we have our first child, (3) a family that has stayed together through the years (almost impossible to achieve without the help of God), and (4) the inclusion of the extended family (cousins, uncles, aunts, grandparents) into the celebration.

I call our son Greg "Christmas Boy," for ever since he left home for the career world, no sooner is one Christmas celebration over than he wants to know where the next one is going to be so he can plan ahead for it. I would guess that a similar love for this most special of seasons can be found everywhere Christmas is celebrated as it should be—keeping in mind Whose birthday we are celebrating.

I, too, have always looked forward to "going home for Christmas." May the good Lord bless and guide you and yours as you, too, travel home for Christmas.

Elizabeth King English

WAITING . . . WAITING FOR CHRISTMAS

Through the years that I have been editing Christmas anthologies, no story has been submitted for possible inclusion more regularly than this one, first printed by Guideposts *over forty years ago. Well, I recently opened an envelope, and lo, here it was again! This time I found it impossible to push it aside.*

Its time has come—the write-in story of the year!

*H*erman and I finally locked our store and dragged ourselves home to South Caldwell Street in Charlotte, North Carolina. It was 11:00 P.M., Christmas Eve of 1949. We were dog tired.

Ours was one of those big old general appliance stores that sold everything from refrigerators and toasters and record players to bicycles and dollhouses and games. We'd sold almost all of our toys; and all of the layaways, except one package, had been picked up.

Usually Herman and I kept the store open until everything had been picked up. We knew we wouldn't have woken up very happy on Christmas morning knowing that some little child's gift was back on the layaway shelf. But the person who had put a dollar down on that package never appeared.

Early Christmas morning our twelve-year-old son, Tom, and Herman and I were out under the tree opening up gifts. But I'll tell you, there was something very humdrum about this Christmas. Tom was growing up; he hadn't wanted any toys—just clothes and games. I missed his childish exuberance of past years.

As soon as breakfast was over, Tom left to visit his friend next door. And Herman disappeared into the bedroom, mumbling, "I'm going back to sleep. There's nothing left to stay up for anyway."

So there I was alone, doing the dishes and feeling very let down. It was nearly 9:00 A.M., and sleet mixed with snow cut the air outside. The wind rattled our windows, and I felt grateful for the warmth of the apartment. *Sure glad I don't have to go out on a day like today,* I thought to myself, picking up the wrappings and ribbons strewn around the living room.

And then it began. Something I'd never experienced before. A strange, persistent urge. "Go to the store," it seemed to say.

I looked at the icy sidewalk outside. *That's crazy,* I said to myself. I tried dismissing the thought, but it wouldn't leave me alone. *Go to the store.*

Well, I *wasn't* going to go. I'd never gone to the store on Christmas Day in all the ten years we'd owned it. No one opened shop on that day. There wasn't any reason to go, I didn't want to, and I wasn't going to.

For an hour, I fought that strange feeling. Finally, I couldn't stand it any longer, and I got dressed.

"Herman," I said, feeling silly, "I think I'll walk down to the store."

Herman woke up with a start. "Whatever for? What are you going to do there?"

"Oh, I don't know," I replied lamely. "There's not much to do here. I just think I'll wander down."

He argued against it a little, but I told him that I'd be back soon. "Well, go on," he grumped, "but I don't see any reason for it."

I put on my gray wool coat and a gray tam on my head, then my galoshes and my red scarf and gloves. Once outside, none of these garments seemed to help. The wind cut right through me and the sleet stung my cheeks. I groped my way along the mile down to 117 East Park Avenue, slipping and sliding all the way.

I shivered, and tucked my hands inside the pockets of my coat to keep them from freezing. I felt ridiculous. I had no business being out in that bitter chill.

There was the store just ahead. The sign announced Radio-Electronics Sales and Service, and the big glass windows jutted out onto the sidewalk. *But, what in the world?* I wondered. In front of the store stood two little boys, huddled together, one about nine, and the other six.

"Here she comes!" yelled the older one. He had his arm around the younger. "See, I told you she would come," he said jubilantly.

The two little children were half frozen. The younger one's face was wet with tears, but when he saw me, his eyes opened wide and his sobbing stopped.

"What are you two children doing out here in this freezing rain?" I scolded, hurrying them into the store and turning up the heat. "You should be at home on a day like this!" They were poorly dressed. They had no hats or gloves, and their shoes barely held together. I rubbed their small, icy hands, and got them up close to the heater.

"We've been waiting for you," replied the older. They had been standing outside since 9:00 A.M., the time I normally open the store.

"Why were you waiting for me?" I asked, astonished.

"My little brother, Jimmy, didn't get any Christmas." He touched Jimmy's shoulder. "We want to buy some skates. That's what he wants. We have these three dollars. See, Miss Lady," he said, pulling the money from his pocket.

I looked at the dollars in his hand. I looked at their expectant faces. And then I looked around the store. "I'm sorry," I said, "but we've sold almost everything. We have no ska—" Then my eye caught sight of the layaway shelf with its one lone package. I tried to remember . . . could it be . . . ?

"Wait a minute," I told the boys. I walked over, picked up the package, unwrapped it and, miracle of miracles, there was a pair of skates!

Jimmy reached for them. *Lord,* I said silently, *let them be his size.*

And miracle added upon miracle, they *were* his size.

When the older boy finished tying the laces on Jimmy's right foot and saw that the skate fit—perfectly— he stood up and presented the dollars to me.

"No, I'm not going to take your money," I told him. I couldn't take his money. "I want you to have these skates, and I want you to use your money to get some gloves for your hands."

The two boys just blinked at first. Then their eyes became like saucers, and their grins stretched wide when they understood I was giving them the skates, and I didn't want their three dollars.

What I saw in Jimmy's eyes was like a blessing. It was pure joy, and it was beautiful. My low spirits rose.

After the children had warmed up, I turned down the heater, and we walked out together. As I locked the door, I turned to the older brother and said, "How lucky that I happened to come along when I did. If you'd stood there much longer, you'd have frozen. But how did you boys know I would come?"

I wasn't prepared for his reply. His gaze was steady, and he answered me softly, "I knew you would come," he said. "I asked Jesus to send you."

The tingles in my spine weren't from the cold, I knew. God had planned this.

As we waved good-bye, I turned home to a brighter Christmas than I had left. Tom brought his friend over to our house. Herman got out of bed; his father, "Papa" English, and sister, Ella, came by. We had a wonderful dinner and a wonderful time.

But the one thing that made that Christmas really wonderful was the one thing that makes every Christmas wonderful—Jesus was there.

Elizabeth King English

Elizabeth King English writes for such contemporary magazines as *Guideposts*.

Mary Agnes Jackman

HIS GUIDING STAR

_____

Toby was completely alone in the world—except for Smiles. And now Smiles had disappeared. What should he do? What could he do?

This old Christmas story is virtually unknown today, but I think you'll agree it needs to live on.

*M*iracles do happen. Toby O'Brien may not have put the thought into words, but the realization of its truth sang through his being as he pressed the puppy closer to his ragged sweater coat. That he, of all the people at the dog show who had looked longingly at the darling little fox terrier, should hold the winning ticket! Something more than chance, this—surely, more than chance.

He hadn't even expected to see the dog show. He had hung about the building all day, selling his papers, watching the dogs go in. Occasionally, he put his grimy fist on the coat of a friendly collie, or he stooped to touch a golden ball of fluff that they called a pom. He had never owned a dog, but he had hoped to have one some day. When a fellow hasn't anyone belonging to him, and a capacity for affection so great that there is a constant hunger in his heart for someone to love, why, the thing to do is to get a dog. When he had money enough he would buy a dog and never be lonesome any more.

The streetlights were going on when he sold a paper to a big fur-coated man who had driven up to the building. "Here, lad, keep an eye on my car till I get my dogs." He came out with two grey-hounds and put them into crates. He handed Toby a dime. Then he fished in his pocket. "Here's a ticket, lad. Pop in and look 'em over. And hang on to your stub. They're drawing for a wire-haired terrier."

Toby thanked him and went in. There was a crowd around a packing case, but Toby, being small and skinny, edged through. A little white and tan dog, washed pink with cleanliness, yipped at him in joyous welcome, blinked brown whiskery eyes, and tried to clamber out to Toby.

Toby exclaimed: "Oh, you beauty! You darling tike!" Then he was pushed aside.

He looked about, sat down and waited. Not that he had anything to wait or hope for.

And—this was the miracle!—Toby held the winning stub.

He could not believe it; even with the little body snuggled warmly in his arms. Even with people clamoring to buy him—"Give you twenty bucks for that puppy, Boy."

"No," Toby replied gravely to each of them. "No. He ain't for sale, I tell you." He got away quickly, his feet feather light with happiness, his lips whispering to his treasure. "What's your name, little feller? I'll call you Smiles. Yes, that's it—Smiles. Listen, Smiles. I won't ever sell you—ever nor never. You were given to me 'cause I ain't got no family. I ain't got nobody at all. But now I've got you, little feller. You're all and everybody I need."

Smiles put out a warm raspy tongue to lick his newfound master's face. A seal it was to the covenant between them.

They had one week of perfect happiness together. Then—I hesitate to speak of this time—Toby lost his dog.

They had been selling papers as usual, the two of them, and business was brisk. Smiles helped. He guarded the pile of papers, and he looked up at passers-by so cunningly, he was quite irresistible. And Toby's face was bright and clean, his manners good, because owning a dog like Smiles, he just had to act like a gentleman.

More than one lady stopped to admire Smiles, and one day, a man, amused by the dog's antics, gave Toby a half dollar tip. Toby spent it extravagantly on a nail-studded collar and Smiles' head went high with pride.

Then, one morning, Toby rushed across the street to sell a paper to a man who beckoned from a car. When he came back, Smiles was gone.

Gone! Oh, no. He must be near somewhere. He couldn't be gone! Toby began to run panic-stricken up and down the street, calling, calling, begging of strangers: "Have you seen my dog? My dog? Smiles—my wee dog—"

A policeman stopped him and took a description of the puppy. People were kind. But kindness couldn't help. Smiles was gone.

Days passed before he gave way completely to the blackness of despair. Food choked him—how could he eat—Smiles might be starving! How could he sleep on his narrow cot, and the little wanderer out in the cold! Tracks in the snow—dogs advertised in the Lost and Found columns—questioning—searching—praying—but never anywhere—never anywhere, the miracle that was Smiles.

Yet still he watched the papers, and once again there was a notice at which his pulses leaped. Should he go, or not? He had been disappointed so often. He could not bear it any more. Yet he must go, because it might be—it might be Smiles.

His quest this time led him to a part of the city that

he'd never seen before. The leaves were off the trees, and although the flowers were gone and there was a whiff of snow, it was like a great park in which were set beautiful palaces. And near one of them, he saw a group of people. A nurse was wheeling an invalid chair in which a boy sat, a thin, dark-eyed boy about his own age. The lower part of his body was wrapped in a plaid rug, and covered as they were, there seemed to be something wrong with his legs. But on the rug, stroked by a gloved hand, rested a white and tan dog—with a nail-studded collar about his neck!

"Smiles!" Toby shouted.

Smiles leaped and ran to him, his whole body wagging in an exuberance of joy. The nurse followed smartly after.

"It's my dog," Toby said defensively. "The little kid had my dog."

"Yes, I believe he is your dog," she answered pleasantly. "Come in with us, and speak to the mistress."

With the dog clutched tight in his arms, he followed. The wide door swung open, and a servant helped with the chair up the steps. "Tell Mrs. Palmer it's a boy to see about the dog," the nurse said to him.

Then a woman came into the hall.

Toby had dreamed about mothers. But never had he imagined anyone just so right as was this mother. The way she looked at the little fellow in the wheelchair— the look that mothers have. She pressed the boy's head against her rough textured yellow dress and stroked his black hair. "Go along with Glover, dear," she whispered, "while I talk to this boy."

13

The child held her by the chain of amber beads. "You know what you promised, Mother—"

"I know, Robert," she soothed him. "Go with Glover, son. I'll get him for you."

If the boy asked for the moon, Toby thought, she'd reach right up and put it into his hand. But it wasn't the moon that Robert wanted, it was his dog. Toby stiffened his will, hardened his heart against them both.

In a bewildering room, she bade Toby sit down on a couch. She sat down too. And Toby couldn't turn his eyes away from the beautiful lady. There were crinkled laughter lines etched about her mouth, and shadows beneath her eyes that told of secret tears. Her hair was black and shining smooth, with two white wings above her temples. And her voice had music in it.

She asked him his name, and he told her. "I suppose you're very much attached to your dog?" she questioned. "He's such a charming little fellow."

"Yes, Ma'am," said Toby, "I am. He's all the family I got."

He felt her eyes traveling over his shabby attire, and he held his good boot over the broken toe cap, and covered the worst hole in his gaping sweater. "What do you call the puppy?" she asked.

"Smiles."

"Why, that's delightful, Toby. Robert couldn't think of a suitable name, but that just fits. We'll keep that name."

Toby gave back her glance, unsmilingly.

"You see, I hope to buy Smiles from you," she continued winsomely. "If you'll put a price on him—I know he's a valuable dog, and I'm sure you can do with the money—why, whatever you ask, I'll double it. Robert would like to have him for his own."

"He's not for sale, Ma'am," Toby replied, firmly. "I told you he's my family and besides, I promised."

"But you can buy another with the money," she argued, "and lots of other things as well. I'll give you plenty—"

Toby broke in on her passionately. "You can buy another dog for Robert," he shrilled. "You can buy hundreds and hundreds of dogs for him. You can buy all the dogs in the world—but you can't buy my dog! He was given to me—to be my family—and I promised—"

She flushed at his outburst, sighed, came over to sit on the couch near him. "That sounds reasonable, Toby. But perhaps if I explain—if I tell you that Robert's a cripple—he's seven years old, and he's never walked. He never will walk. How old are you, Toby?"

"Goin' on ten, I am," Toby answered.

"Well, maybe you won't understand what it means to be partly paralyzed, helpless, different from other boys. And Robert has always been simply terrified of animals. If a dog suddenly jumped up on him he'd suffer a perfect paroxysm of fear. I suppose that sounds absurd to you?"

"Oh, well, ma'am," Toby conceded, "in a little shaver, and crippled—"

"We've tried to help him overcome this fear. But without success. Until one day Glover had him in the park. They saw a mean looking man skulking along with a pup under his arm. A policeman appeared, and the thief—he was a thief, I guess—dropped the dog, kicked him, and the pup ran straight to Robert's arms.

And Robert caught him—held him—all his protective sense aroused. And they just loved each other. So now you see why—for he's still afraid of other animals. Robert needs the dog more than you do, Toby. Please say you'll sell him."

Toby swallowed hard. "No!" he said loudly. "No! I ain't a-goin' to. Not ever. Not for no one. I promised."

She touched a bell and a maid entered. "There's a roll of bills in my dressing case, Marie. Bring it to me, please."

But Toby bolted past her, with Smiles held tight. "Let me out of here," he choked. "Let me out, I say. She's trying to snitch my dog!"

They were at home again together, Toby and his dog. But not happy like they had been before. Their rapturous delight in each other was gone.

For one thing, Toby had to leave Smiles in the day time shut up in his basement room. For Smiles was uneasy and discontented, and Toby dared not risk losing him again. And at night, Smiles, looking up at the high window, would cry and whimper, and Toby, twisting and squirming on his hard bed would mutter: "He's thinking of the poor little rich kid. But—that kid has everything in the world—and I've only got—my dog."

It was getting near to Christmas, too, and the very spirit of Christmas filled the air. Christmas stories. Christmas gifts. Christmas giving. Well, he had no one to give to; nothing to give. Christmas didn't mean a thing to him. Except that people were more generous. "Keep the change, young'un, for Christmas." Queer how happy they seemed, giving at Christmas time.

Well, he had no folks to give to—he said it often—and nothing at all to give. Was he a little rich boy with parents and a home and all his heart desired? No; he was not; and he hadn't anything to give. He hugged Smiles until the dog protested, half in pain. And was it his fault that the little shaver was crippled? Still, it must be fierce not to walk—and not to have a dog. He knew how terrible it was to have a dog, and love him, and then to have him taken away. But—why should he feel sorry for the poor little rich kid!

He walked a good deal at nights with Smiles by his side, and wondered why he walked. And all about in the churches he heard people singing: "Peace on earth, Goodwill to men." Things like that. Only Christmas didn't mean a thing to him.

But on Christmas Day itself, the struggle ended. The decision seemed to be taken right out of his hands. There was only one thing a fellow could do.

He dressed carefully, groomed Smiles pink with cleanliness, and went on his way.

Outside the mansion he stopped to feast his home hungry heart on the picture within: windows gay with holly wreaths, a tree, star-topped, and a family group inside it. Robert reclining in a low chair; his parents winding toys to amuse the weary languid child. Toby felt almost contemptuous of their efforts—as if things of wood and wire could satisfy a boy! He ascended the steps quickly, and lifted the knocker.

The door swung open. Smiles darted out of sight. "Goodbye, Smiles." The faintest whisper, the barest gesture of farewell. Then, set little mouth puckered to a whistle, brave feet blind on the steps, Toby turned away.

"Oh, Toby. Toby O'Brien." The beautiful lady calling him. "How nice of you to visit us on Christmas Day."

"Yes, ma'am." How warm the house was, and the scent of roses everywhere. "I had to come. To bring the little kid his dog." Toby turned his snow-wet cap round and round in frost-chapped hands. "I kept a-thinkin'. I just couldn't stand it. Here's me with legs and everything. And he's not got—even a dog."

She touched his wet sleeve. "But you said you wouldn't sell him?"

"Sell him! I ain't a-sellin' him. But I guess I can give him away without breakin' nary a promise—Christmas and all—"

"Robert will be very happy. Come in and tell him."

Mr. Palmer said cheerily as he entered the firelit room: "Merry Christmas, Toby."

"Merry Christmas, sir," Toby replied, mindful of his manners.

"Robert, dear," Mrs. Palmer said, "Toby has brought Smiles to you to keep. Isn't that wonderful?"

Over Robert's face flashed a beam of joy; then he sobered. "It's very kind of you." He smiled gallantly. "But I'm afraid I can't accept. You see, Mother's been talking to me. That Smiles is all the family you've got. So of course I couldn't take him. Thank you very much."

"But you've just got to take him," Toby insisted, bewildered. "You've *just got* to. It's Christmas, and when you're given a Christmas present, why, you've got to take it."

"Is that right, Mother?" Robert asked, relaxing with a sigh.

"I believe it is, son. I believe that's Christmas etiquette."

"Oh well—in that case. Come, Smiles. Up. Up. Right here, old boy." The little dog leaped, licked his face, and snuggled down to be petted. Mr. Palmer tiptoed to the door; beckoned to the beautiful lady. The boys were left alone together.

They were shy of one another at first, shy and awkward, but Smiles, frisky and full of tricks, drew them together, and the room soon rang with laughter. Robert's eyes sparkled, his cheeks glowed.

"Wow, Toby," he said, "this is the best Christmas I've ever had. It's the most fun I've ever had in all my life."

"Same here," Toby replied, enthusiastically. But he was quick to see that Robert had played long enough. He hadn't much strength.

"I guess I'll be getting along now." Smiles pricked up his ears, ready for departure too. Toby whispered, "Coax him out to the back, and I'll sneak away. And don't ever lose him. He'll soon forget about me."

Robert went out propelling the wheeled chair, Smiles riding on his shoulder, barking at Toby to come along and play this new game.

Toby picked up his cap and mittens, and went softly across the rugs to the great hall. There Mrs. Palmer came to him.

"Sit down again, Toby." She placed him once more

on the downy couch, piled cushions at his back. She touched a button and a tree twinkled with a hundred colored candle lights. At the very top, the silver star rayed out a new effulgence, glowing, like the star of Bethlehem. Toby's eyes were fixed upon it.

"You know about Christmas, Toby?" Mrs. Palmer asked.

"Oh, yes, ma'am. I seen the pictures. The Shepherds and the Star. The angels. 'And unto us is born this day—' I read about it in the papers."

"You can read, then?"

"Oh, yes. I been to school some, and I learn myself, nights."

"Robert has a governess," Mrs. Palmer said. She turned the rings on her fingers; the stones caught the light and shot darts of fire. "He doesn't like lessons much. It's hard for a boy to study alone."

"Yes, ma'am," Toby agreed. "I know how it is."

She was silent for a while. "You never knew your mother, Toby?"

"No, ma'am."

"She would have been very proud of you this day, dear boy. Don't think I don't know what it cost you giving Smiles up—all you had. I hope your mother knows."

She went on after a while. "It's queer about mothers. All they ask in life is to see their children happy. And sometimes that is beyond their power. Now Robert— there's nothing we would not do for him. But he's often unhappy, shut off in his little soul. Smiles will do him a world of good—but he needs human companionship— he needs a boy's companionship, too."

"For years we've talked of adopting a boy. We've tried, but—you see, Robert's brother will need to be a boy of rather exceptional character. One capable of—of big things. If I could find him, he would share and share alike with Robert—even to my love."

Toby, trembling, his heart going thump-thump, his breath choked in his throat—"And Smiles did adopt you both, didn't he?"

She was smiling at him through tears.

"Oh, Toby, I'm so long in getting to the point. I'm so afraid you'll turn me down. But wouldn't you let us give you our name? Stay here with us always? Share Smiles' affection? Be a brother to Robert—"

His head whirled. He held on to her hand like grim death. If he once let go he'd go floating up, up—

Her voice came faint as from a far distance—

"And unto us, a son?"

Toby had reached Home.

Mary Agnes Jackman

Mary Agnes Jackman wrote during the early part of the twentieth century for family magazines in Canada and the United States.

Agnes Sligh Turnbull

HOLLY AT THE DOOR

Somewhere through the years—she knew not how or when—love had gone. So had respect—even civility. And now it was Christmas. But even in this most sentimental of seasons, there was no love, no kindness, in the Barton household. Just biting sarcasm and stifling selfishness.

But how could love be retained when Alice didn't know how or when it had been lost?

On the outside—that is, in the smart little suburban town of Branchbrook—Christmas week had begun most auspiciously. A light fall of snow made the whole place look like an old-fashioned holiday greeting card; the neat English stuccos and Colonial clapboards, set back in wide lawns, seemed to gather their flocks of clipped little pine and spruce shrubbery closer to them and suggest through their fresh curtained windows the thought of bright wood fires and mistletoe and shining Christmas cheer soon to come.

In the parish room of St. Andrew's small gray stone church the children were practicing carols while pigeons cooed on the roof. And down in the village center great boxes of holly wreaths stood in the street before all the grocery store windows, and bevies of slender little virgin pine trees, ready and waiting for the great moment to which they had been born, leaned against all the shop door-ways.

The postman smiled beneath his staggering load, thinking of later benefactions; and the windows of Beverly's Fine Food Stuffs, the town's most exclusive market, were caparisoned with every delicacy which even a Christmas epicure might desire.

Strangers spoke to each other, children laughed gleefully, shop men made jokes with their customers, everybody was busy, friendly, somehow relaxed from the ordinary conventional aloofness, because Christmas was only five days away. Everything was just as it should be, on the outside.

But on the inside—that is to say, in the big Colonial home of the Bartons which had been built just long enough before prices went up to make it seem now more of an abode of wealth than it really was—here the week had begun in the worst way possible. Monday morning had started with a quarrel.

Alice Barton had not rested well the night before. She had fully planned to spend all Sunday afternoon and evening addressing Christmas cards. That would have seen them all safely in the postman's hands this morning.

But the plan had been frustrated by the Levitts dropping in for a call, staying to tea and spending the evening. And it had been Tom's fault entirely. He was the one that simply kept them. Of course she had to be decently polite. They sat listening to the radio until eleven. After that she had been too tired to start the cards. And here they were all to do now, this morning, more than a hundred of them, on top of all the regular day's work and the committee meeting at eleven. And she must get a few more hours of shopping in! That would be hectic now but there was no help for it. And all her packages were yet to be tied up, and Mrs. Dunlop's bridge-luncheon on Wednesday and Catherine's friend coming Thursday! She *must* not forget about the guest room curtains! Why had she let Catherine have anyone come at Christmas time!

The dull headache she had when she rose became a splitting pain. She scarcely spoke to Tom as she dressed except for one brief and fitting retort to his: "Now don't spend all day in the bathroom. I have to shave!"

She went downstairs, mechanically checking off the things she must tell Delia, the maid.

Tom was down before the children. He opened the front door for the newspaper which Delia always forgot to bring in and came toward the table with his brows drawn. It was not a propitious moment, but the thing had to be done.

"Tom."

"Darned if they haven't given that murderer another reprieve! How do they ever expect to have . . ."

"Listen, Tom! There's something I want to ask you."

"A pretty kind of justice! Wrap all the little murderers up in pink wool blankets for fear they get cold in the neck, and forget the poor cuss that's been killed! You know, Alice, what ought to be done is this. . . ."

"Yes, but Tom, listen. I'll simply have to have a little more money!" (It was dreadful to have to ask him now when he was all stirred up over this thing in the paper!) "I'll just have to do some more shopping, just a few little things I forgot, and I'd rather be free to go about instead of sticking to the charge accounts. If you could give me . . ."

Tom was suddenly all attention. His dark eyes were looking at her keenly. He broke in.

"Why, I gave you an extra twenty-five last Friday."

"I know, Tom, but it took every cent of it for the cards. And even then I had to spend most of the day trying to find respectable ones within my price." Tom's face looked thunderous.

"Do you mean to tell me that it takes *twenty-five dollars* now to send out Christmas cards? *Twenty-five dollars!* Confound it, that would buy two tons of coal. That's the sheerest piece of criminal waste I ever heard of!"

Alice's face darkened too. "Well, what are you going to do about it? You know the kind everybody sends us. We can't look like pikers. It would have cost fifty dollars to get the engraved kind I wanted. I won't send out cheap stereotyped ones, so all that's left for me is to try to pick out something artistic and individual, at least for the people we care most about. It's no easy job, and this is the thanks I get!"

"You bet you'll get none from me. Do you know how I feel? I hate Christmas! Nothing but money, money beforehand, and nothing but bills, bills, bills afterward. It's enough to drive a man crazy. And what's the sense of it? You send a lot of cards to people that barely look at 'em and throw 'em in the fire! You women exchange a bunch of junk that you never use. And as a family, we spend like drunken sailors on a lot of extravagant things we've no business having. And old Dad, poor boob, gets a good dinner out of it and then he pays and pays and pays for the next six months! That's the way I've got it doped out!"

Alice's face was frozen in sharp lines. "If that's the way you feel about it I suppose I needn't hope for my coat."

"Coat! What coat?"

"Tom, as if you didn't know perfectly well what I wanted this year more than anything. The short fur coat! Why I've talked about it all fall. I think every woman in town has one but me. I can't wear my big seal one shopping and marketing! And my cloth one is simply gone! Why, I thought all the time you knew, and that you'd surely . . ." There were almost tears in her voice.

"So it's come to that, has it! A woman has to have a special kind of fur coat to do her marketing in! Too bad! Well, I'm sorry to disappoint you but you can't bank on one this year—unless you'd like to mortgage the house!"

He got up abruptly from the table. Young Tom and Catherine had just come into the dining room in time for the last speech. They looked at their parents with cool, amused eyes. It was not the first quarrel they had witnessed in the last years since they had left childhood behind. Catherine, a day pupil at Miss Bossart's finishing school, and young Tom, a senior in high school, were startlingly mature. They were calmer, more cynical, more unemotional than their parents. They touched life with knowing fingers that never trembled. Alice marveled at them.

She rose now too and followed Tom into the library. He sat down a moment at the desk and then flicked her a slip of paper.

"There's fifty. And that's all, remember, until next month's allowance!"

Alice's voice was like cold steel. "Thanks. I'm sure I'll enjoy spending it since it's so very generously given."

Tom did not answer. He got into his overcoat, called a general good-by and left the house.

Alice came back to the children. Young Tom looked up quizzically. "Well, Mums, that ought to hold him for a while, eh, what?" he remarked as he helped himself hugely to the omelette.

Catherine's brows were slightly puckered. "Say, Mother, am I going to get my watch? Dad was in such a vile humor, I'm scared. Really I'll feel like a pauper down there at Miss Bossart's unless I get something a little bit flossy. And this old watch I've had since I was twelve. There isn't another round gold one in school. Everything's platinum now! Really, it's not much to ask for compared to what most of the girls are getting. Jean and Hilda know they're getting cars of their own! And flocks of them are getting marvelous fur coats."

"Well, you have your new coat," Alice reminded her.

"Oh, yes," Catherine agreed with a faint deprecating sigh, "such as it is."

Alice opened her lips for a quick remonstrance and closed them again. Oh, what was the use! The children were always ungrateful. They had no real appreciation these days of what their parents gave them. With them it was take, take, take, and never a thought of value received.

Young Tom looked up from his toast and marmalade with his most winning smile.

"Say, Mums, can you let me have a fiver out of your new pile? I'm in the very dickens of a hole."

Alice fastened quick eyes upon him. "Where has your allowance gone!" she asked sharply.

"Well, Mums, it's so small to begin with I can hardly see it, and then just now round Christmas time there's always such a darned lot of extras!"

Catherine cut in sweetly: "Such as bouquets of orchids for Miss Doris Kane!"

"*Orchids!*" Alice almost screamed the word. "Tom, you don't mean for a minute to tell me you're sending orchids to a girl! High school children sending orchids! I never in my life heard of anything so wickedly absurd!"

"Well, Mums, what are you going to do? That's what all the girls want now for the dances, and a fellow can't look like a piker! I've got to order some for tonight. Lend me five, won't you, just to tide me over? What we ought to have is a charge account at the florist's. That's what all the other fellows' folks have."

"No doubt," Alice said sarcastically. "It's barely possible that some of your friends' fathers may have more money to pay their bills than your father has. But I suppose you never thought of that! Well, I'll give you five this time, but I don't want you ever to ask me again for such a purpose."

"And now if he's through," Catherine broke in, "what about me? Is there any reason why I should be broke while my handsome young brother sends orchids to Doris Kane? You should see what the girls are giving each other for Christmas. It makes me sick to hand out the things I have. They look like a rummage sale compared with the rest! I did want one decent thing for Jean, but I'm terribly short."

She looked at her mother challengingly.

Alice made a desperate gesture with her hands. "All right," she said, "you can have it. Of course it doesn't matter whether I'm short or not! I'm at the place where I don't care much what happens!"

Her head throbbed miserably as she borrowed the two five-dollar bills from her housekeeping purse and gave them to the children. She had a vivid perception that each thought they should have been tens. Their thanks were scant and careless. They had only received their just due, and scarcely that!

Alice felt sick as she climbed the stairs to the den where she kept her desk. Now for the cards. Christmas was a hard, trying time. She would be glad when it was over.

She began in frantic haste, selecting, addressing, searching her note book and the telephone directory for streets and numbers. Five, ten, fifteen finished, stamped, ready.

Suddenly she picked up an alien from the carefully chosen mass that lay about her, a cheap little card that she knew she had never bought. Either she or the sales girl must have caught it up by mistake with some of the others. It was a commonplace little card of the folder variety that carries a sentimental verse inside. Alice opened it mechanically before tossing it into the waste basket. And there beneath her eyes were these words:

Oh what, my dear, of Christmas cheer could any one
*   wish more,*
Than candle-light and you within, and holly at the door!

She stared at the words unbelievingly. Not for thirty years had she thought of that old song. And now suddenly she heard it in her father's voice, just as he used to sing it Christmas after Christmas as he went through the house with his hammer in one hand and a dangling bough of green in the other.

And holly at the door, and holly at the door!
With candle-light and you within, and holly at the door!

She hummed the old melody under her breath, and then she found herself bending over the desk, face in hands, weeping, while over her swept great waves of homesickness, poignant pangs of yearning for a place and a time that had drifted out of her consciousness.

At last she raised her head and leaned it against the high back of the chair. It seemed almost as though invisible fingers had pressed it there, had closed her eyes, had made the pen drop from her passive hand. All at once she was back in the little town of her childhood where she had not been, and where not even her mind had traveled vividly, these long years.

Christmas time in Martinsville! Christmas in the small frame house that had been home. Mother singing blithely as she stuffed the turkey in the kitchen. Father standing proudly by, watching her every movement. For the turkey was an event. One turkey a year, to be ordered after due consideration from one of the farmers near town, to be received with a small flurry of excitement when it arrived and to be picked and prepared for the oven by Mother's own skillful fingers.

"I suppose we should ask Miss Amanda for dinner tomorrow. The Smiths usually have her but they're away this year," Mother was saying.

Father agreed. "Maybe we'd better. It's not nice to think of anybody sitting down all by themselves to a cold bite on Christmas!"

"When we have so much," Mother went on. "You'd better stop and ask her when you go for the mail tonight."

Footsteps on the porch. Father and Mother break into smiles. "There's Alice," they exclaim in unison.

Quick stamping of snow on the scraper, quick opening of the door, a quick rush of cold wind and a quick, joyous child's voice.

"Mother, the holly's come; Father, look at this! Isn't it lovely! Mr. Harris just got in now with the wagon from Wanesburg. And he brought a big box of it. He has wreaths, too, but they're a quarter apiece. I think this bunch is prettier and it was only a dime. Look at the berries!"

The child's cheeks are as scarlet as her red toboggan and sweater that Mother herself had knitted. Her blue eyes are shining and eager, her light hair tossed by the wind.

"Put it up quick, Father, and I'll get the red ribbon for it." She flies up stairs, stumbling in her haste.

Suddenly, laughter below, expostulation, hurrying feet in the front hall. "Alice, Alice, don't open the under drawer of my bureau! You *didn't,* did you? Mercy, we had such a scare! The ribbon's in the top drawer, left hand side. Now mind, no looking any-where else!"

"And holly at the door . . ."

Father's big voice booming out happily.

Alice skips down the stairs. "I never peeped! Honestly. But what can it be you have for me? It's something to wear! Oh, I can't wait."

"And holly at the door . . ."

Father's hammer tapping smartly, then the gay swing-ing green branch with its brave little bow of red. They all have to go out to admire it.

"And, Father, you should see the church! It's won-derful this year. George Davis and Mr. Parmley climbed up on two ladders and tied the greens to the big cross rafter and fastened a silver star right at the top. It's never been so pretty. And the tree! Mother, it reaches the ceiling! And Mrs. Davis was putting little white lambs under it and shepherds. We saw it when we were there practicing for tonight. Oh, I *hope* I don't forget my speech."

Immediately, concentrated, proud interest. Father and Mother sit down to listen once again. Alice stands in front of the table, her hands primly by her sides, her face upraised in gentle seriousness.

The milk-white sheep looked up one night,
And there stood an angel all in white,
And though he spoke no words to them,
He was there on the hill of Bethlehem,
That very first Christmas morning!

The lowing cattle meekly stood
Near to a manger rough and rude. . . .

On and on goes the sweet childish voice to the end.

And the time will come, so the wise men say,
When the wolf and the lamb together shall play,
And a little child shall lead the way,
The child of that first Christmas morning.

"Pshaw!" says Father, poking the fire to hide the tender mist in his eyes. "You couldn't forget that if you tried!"

"Of course you couldn't," Mother reassures. "Only remember to speak loud enough that they can hear you in the back of the church!"

"And all the girls have new dresses," Alice exclaims, coming excitedly down to earth again. "And I said I had one too. That wasn't a fib, was it, Mother? It really is new, for me, even if it is Aunt Jennie's old one dyed."

"Of course," Mother stoutly agrees. "And all the

trimmings are new. That light cashmere certainly took the dye well."

"I don't see how you got it in such a beautiful shade of red. It's just like the holly!"

"You must remember, my dear," Father puts in with loving pride, "that your mother is a very wonderful person."

The soft early dusk of Christmas Eve falls upon Martinsville. Father starts down to the post-office for the mail. Mother prepares a light supper to be eaten in the kitchen because of the general haste. For the big Sunday School entertainment and "treat" is at seven-thirty. Alice sets out with her small pail to go to a neighbor's for the daily supply of milk.

It is so still in the village street. All white and hushed. Just a little stirring like wings in the church yard pines. The child stops, breathless, clasping her hands to her breast, the small pail dangling unheeded, her whole tender young soul caught up suddenly in a white mystery. Christmas Eve! The baby in the manger. The gold stars looking down just as they were tonight, and the angels sweeping through the sky on soft shining wings, singing, *singing*.

It seemed almost as though they would appear any moment there where the stars were brightest, right back of the church steeple.

Why, it was real. It was true! Christmas Eve was happening again, within her, down deep, deep in her heart somewhere, as she stood there all quiet and alone in the snow. The wonderful aching beauty of it! It was as though she and the big wide star-swept night had a secret together. Or perhaps it was she *and God*.

Down the street comes a quick, clear jingle-jangle-jingle. A sleigh has just turned the corner. Alice starts and runs the rest of the way to the neighbors!

"And two quarts, please, Mother says, if you can spare it, because tomorrow's Christmas!"

She is dressed for the entertainment in the new dyed dress, her long curls showing golden above its rich red. Father and Mother suddenly begin to consult together in low voices in the kitchen. They come out at last impressively.

"Would she rather have one of her presents, not the big one but the other one, now, so she could wear it tonight? Would she?"

Alice stands considering delightedly, blue eyes like stars. "The big present would still be left for tomorrow?" she queries eagerly.

"You bet!" Father assures her.

"Then—I believe—I'll take the other—*now!*"

Mother brings it out. A hair ribbon! Just the color of the dress. Bigger and broader than any she has ever had. It is finally perched like a scarlet tanager above the golden curls!

There is the sound of talking, laughing voices passing outside. Scrunch, scrunch, scrunch, of many feet in the snow. People going to the entertainment. The little church up the street is all alight. It is time to go! They start out in the fresh, frosty air. Father follows her and Mother along the narrow snowy path, humming the Holly Song softly to himself.

All at once there was a shrill persistent ringing. It was not of a church bell or passing sleighs. It kept on ringing. The woman in the chair before the desk littered with Christmas cards came slowly back to her surroundings. She grasped the telephone dazedly. "This is Mrs. Barton. What meeting! . . . Oh, yes. . . . No, I can't come. . . . I'm—I'm not well."

She hung up the receiver abruptly. The Committee meeting at eleven! It seemed suddenly far away. Her one longing was to get back again to the past where she had just now been living; to those fresh, sweet realities of long ago. She closed her eyes, terrified lest the illusion was lost completely. But slowly, softly, surely, the little snowy village of Martinsville closed in again around her. She was once more the child, Alice.

She was falling asleep on Christmas Eve. The entertainment had been wonderful. She hadn't forgotten her speech, not a word, and the girls all thought her dress was lovely and her hair ribbon had felt so big and pretty and floppy on her head, and the Ladies Quartette had sung "O Holy Night" for a surprise. Nobody knew they had been practicing, and it was so beautiful it had hurt her inside. And the treat candy had ever so many more chocolates in it than last year, and it was snowing again and she could hear the faint jingle-jangle-jingle of the sleighs still going up and down Main Street, and she was so happy! And tomorrow would really be Christmas.

Then all at once it was morning. Father and Mother were talking in low, happy voices in their room. She could hear Father creaking softly down the back stairs to start the fire before she got awake. The stockings would be all filled. Goodness, it was hard to wait.

Then at last a great noise in the front hall. Father shouting, "Merry Christmas! My Christmas gift! Merry Christmas up there!"

It is time now. She flings her chill little body into her red wrapper and slippers and scurries down the stairs. A big fire in the grate! The three big bulging stockings! Father and Mother stand by until she empties hers first. She feels it with delicious caution. Oranges, apples and nuts in the toe. A funny little bumpy thing above. That would be one of Father's jokes. But at the top a mysterious soft, swashy package! She withdraws it slowly. She opens one tiny corner, gasps, opens a little more. Then gives a shrill cry. *"Mother! It couldn't be a muff!"*

She pulls it out, amazed ecstasy on her face. "It *is* a muff! Oh, Father, to think of your getting me a muff." She clasps the small scrap of cheap fur to her breast. "Oh, Mother, I never was so happy."

A subdued sound drew louder, became a sharp rap at the door. Martinsville receded. The woman in the chair opened her eyes with a dull realization of the present. Delia stood in the doorway, dark and ominous. "What about them bed-room curtains?" she demanded.

Alice Barton rose slowly. With a great effort she brought her mind back to the problems of the day. She led the way to the guest room with Delia after her, grumbling inaudibly. Perhaps her eyes were still misted over with sweet memories, for somehow the curtains did not look so bad. "We'll let them go as they are, Delia. You have enough extras to do."

Delia departed in pleased surprise, and Alice sat down in the quiet room before a mirror, and peered into it. Almost she expected to see the child she had once been, the tender, smiling young mouth, the soft, eager eyes, the tumbled curls.

Instead she saw a middle-aged face with all the spontaneous light gone out of it. There were hard lines in it which no amount of expensive "facials" had been able to smooth away. There was a bitter, unlovely droop to the lips.

Alice regarded herself steadily. Where along the way had she lost the spirit of that child who had this day come back to her?

The outward changes of her life passed in review. It was soon after that last happy Christmas in Martinsville that the little town had been swept by disease. The old village doctor had neither knowledge nor equipment to restrain it. When it was over, many homes had been desolated, and Alice, a bewildered little orphan, had gone to Aunt Jennie's in the city.

The changed way of living had been at first startling and then strangely commonplace. She had been fluidly adaptable. She had gone to a fashionable finishing school, had made a smart début, had met Tom, fallen deeply in love and then married him with all the circumstance Aunt Jennie had ordained.

Then had come life in Branchbrook and the beginning for herself of the curious nameless game Aunt Jennie had taught her, of belonging, of keeping up with most; of being ahead of many. A game with no noticeable beginning and no possible end. And of course one had to keep on playing it, for if one stopped it meant being dropped. Life would be insupportable after that.

And yet, would it? The game wasn't making any of them happy as it was. Back in her own restless home she saw again Father and Mother and the little girl named Alice. They had all been so joyously content with each other, had found life with its few small pleasures so wholesome and sweet to the taste.

The woman rose trembling to her feet. Suppose she stopped playing the game! Suppose she didn't care whether she belonged or not. What if she tried walking in the simple ways of her mother?

She stood there thinking in new terms, startled out of all her old standards, crying out to the past to guide her. And then suddenly she raised her arms above her head in a gesture of emancipation.

She examined her extra shopping list for which she had asked the money that morning. All the items were expensive courtesies that need not be rendered if considered apart from the game. She crossed them out one by one.

All that day as she went about her duties, she was conscious of an invisible companion: a child with eager, happy eyes walked beside her, watched her as she helped Delia with the big fruit cake, as she fastened a bough of holly to the door with her own hands.

The child was still close to her in the shadows when she lighted the tall candelabra at dusk and drew the tea-table to the fireside. Just the fire-light and candle-shine to greet Tom when he came. She sat very still on the big divan, waiting. Would he feel the new quiet that possessed her? Would he forgive her for having made all the other Christmases times of confusion and worry? She wondered.

The children were not home yet when Tom came. He hung his coat in the hall closet and entered the living room heavily. He looked tired. His glance swept over the tall lighted candles, and the shining tea table. "What's coming off here? A tea-fight?" he said.

Alice stretched her hands toward him.

"You are the only guest, Tom. You and the children."

The man came nearer in surprise, caught her hands, peered into her face. Then his own softened. "What is it?" he asked.

They sank down together on the divan, hands still clasped tightly, something old and yet new, flooding back and forth between them.

"What is it?" Tom asked again. "There is something . . . tell me."

And then suddenly the woman knew that into her own hard faded eyes there had come again the gladness of youth.

"I had a visit today," she said slowly, "from a little girl of thirty years ago. A little girl I had forgotten. She brought me something precious."

Tom looked at her wonderingly. "Will she come *again? Often?*" he begged.

Alice shook her head and smiled. "There is no need," she answered softly. "For she and her gift have come to stay!"

Agnes Sligh Turnbull
1888–1982

Agnes Sligh Turnbull, author of bestsellers such as *The Bishop's Mantle* (1947), *The Town of Glory* (1952), and *The Golden Journey* (1955), wrote of a world in which values were crucial. Critics might accuse her of lacking realism, but she always maintained that her books and stories mirrored the gentler world she grew up in—a world she felt had much to teach us in our frantic-paced society.

Maud Tousey Fangel

Nancy N. Rue

CHRISTMAS IS FOR KIDS

Or So I Thought Until . . .

Jill, a budding actress in the high school play, felt too overwhelmed by overwork to appreciate Christmas. Christmas was a kid thing anyhow. But that was before T. R. railroaded her into being an angel in a church nativity play.

I sat at the breakfast table that Saturday morning in front of a wall of newspapers. My dad was safely tucked behind the financial page, and my mom had her face in the Styles section. The only way I knew they were there was that Dad gave the occasional grunt, and Mom was gurgling. She was actually gurgling.

"I can't believe it!" she—yes—gurgled. "Marvin Shields has done a review of your play, Jill!" She nudged my father, who grunted twice. "Listen to this!" she said. " 'Cameron High has a fine reputation for its drama program, but it outshone itself last night in the final performance of *Grease.*' "

I really should've been jazzed that a critic from the newspaper had come to see our high school play and put us in the Styles section. I should have been even happier that my dad actually pulled his eyes away from the Dow Jones averages to listen. But I just kept pushing soggy Cheerios around in my bowl with a spoon.

"Oh, Jill!" Mom suddenly squealed. "Listen, listen, listen! 'In addition to spotlighting its magnificent seniors, the Cameron drama program has discovered a rising star in freshman Jill Breckenridge. This shiny-haired, willowy youngster played a relatively minor role in the production but promises to be one of the program's power-houses in the next three years.' " Two pairs of eyes came up over the tops of their papers and shone at me.

"What about that, Darlin'?" Mom said.

"Cool," I said.

"I have to be sure I'll have enough copies of this to send to—oh, I can put them in with the Christmas cards—I'm glad I haven't finished them all yet—"

And with that, Mom disappeared from the breakfast table to make phone calls to everyone she knew who subscribed to the *Cameron Times,* telling them to get their scissors out. She didn't notice that I just went back to toying with my breakfast cereal.

"Well, how 'bout that, huh?" Dad said. His eyes, usually tired behind his glasses, were sparkling at me.

"Yeah, it's cool," I said.

His eyebrows shot up. "Just another review in the whirlwind life of an actress?"

"No." I let the spoon clatter into the bowl and looked at it miserably. "I just didn't know it was going to be this much work. We had so many rehearsals—especially that last week—and this morning we have to go up and strike the set—and I have a big English project due right after vacation that I haven't even started on because I've been doing the play, so I'll have to spend my whole Christmas break doing that—"

I stopped. Dad's eyes had shifted back to Dow Jones. "Welcome to the adult world, Sugar," he said.

Thanks, Dad, I thought. *I feel a lot better now.*

He evaporated behind the newspaper again, and I stared glumly at the back of it. Both pages were dancing with ads about Christmas sales and holiday specials. I almost moaned out loud.

'TIS THE SEASON

Christmas. That was another thing. I hadn't bought the first present. I hadn't even tasted any of the home-made fudge I knew was stacked in the big Tupperware thing on top of the refrigerator. In fact, until that moment, I hadn't noticed that the Christmas place mats were out, and that I had been eating off a snowman.

I looked down at his faded plastic face. My mother's Aunt Annette had spent Christmas with us when I was 7, and I could still remember her looking at that place mat and saying, "Christmas is really for the kids."

Dad grunted again now. "The merchants are sweating it," he mumbled. "Sales are down this season."

I sighed into my dish of disintegrated Cheerios. Aunt Annette was probably right. *Welcome to the adult world, Jill.*

LESSONS FROM A SENIOR

It took us almost until noon to strike the set, mostly because people had to keep stopping to hug and tell each other one more time how incredible we'd been. I was standing at the bottom of a ladder taking the lighting instruments T. R. was handing down to me when the people who were putting away props started singing Christmas carols.

"Oh, man," I moaned.

"What's the matter, Scrooge?" T. R. said from several rungs up the ladder. Her name was actually Tawny Rose, but when people called her that she usually threatened them with bodily harm. She had been our stage manager, and she was a tough senior with blue eyes that riveted you. I didn't want to mess with her.

"What's up?" she asked again.

"About the last thing I want to think about is Christmas," I said.

She snickered as she went at the instrument with a wrench. "Terrific. You're the only other Christian in this cast besides me, and now you're telling me you want to give up Christmas."

"I don't want to give it up. I just—"

She handed me the instrument and climbed down the ladder.

"Let's move this one more time—last one."

I grabbed the other side of the ladder and lifted. "I've figured out the whole celebration thing is for little kids, anyway," I said as we moved stage-right. "I used to wonder why adults got so stressed out during the holidays, and now I know. We just don't have time for it."

T. R. set the ladder down and grunted. She almost sounded like my father. "Let's get this last one down, and then I'm out of here. I have another rehearsal this afternoon."

"What for?" I said.

"The pageant."

"What pageant?"

She looked down at me from atop the ladder. "At our church, Einstein," she said. "Didn't you ever play an angel or a shepherd or whatever?"

I snorted. "No. I wanted to be an angel, but I never got to. They always made me be a cow."

"Poor baby," she said unsympathetically.

"Why do you have to go to their rehearsal?" I said. "I thought it was the little kids' pageant."

"A few of us from youth group are helping. We didn't ask you because you seemed so stressed over this."

I nodded and took the light she handed me. The prop people started in on their fifth chorus of "Joy to the World."

"Don't quit your day jobs!" T. R. yelled to them.

Then she riveted her blue eyes down at me. "Why don't you join in?" she said. "Maybe you could drown them out."

Because it's lame and childish, I wanted to say. But I just shook my head.

YOU WANT ME?

I was reading *Great Expectations* that night with my eyelids at half-mast when the phone rang. It was T. R. still using her stage manager voice.

"Breckenridge," she said, "you coming to church tomorrow?"

"Uh—yeah, of course—"

"Meet me in the big Sunday school room at 9 A.M. Gabriel can't make it, and we need somebody."

I mentally flipped through the youth group roster. "Who's Gabriel?" I asked.

There was a grunt on the other end of the line. "He's the archangel, Einstein. All you have to do is stand on a stool behind the manger and say a couple of lines."

I stared into the receiver. "You mean you want me to be *in* the pageant? With the little kids?"

"You got it," she said, then added, "Bring a sheet."

Before I could even protest—or ask if she wanted fitted or flat—she hung up.

JOB DESCRIPTION OF AN ANGEL

Maybe it was because I was so used to taking orders from T. R. that I showed up in the big Sunday school room the next morning. I was immediately up to my knees in very short humanity with shrill voices all screaming things like "Where's my tail?" and "I have to go potty!"

T. R. found me and yanked the sheet out of my hand.

"All right," she said as she whipped it around my hips and up over my shoulder. I was glad I hadn't gone for the fitted one with the hot-air balloons printed on it. "All you have to do is stand there and look like the head angel. When they uncover the baby Jesus' face, you say, 'Glory to God in the highest'—you know the rest."

I nodded numbly as she pushed a safety pin into place at my shoulder and patted it. "Oh," she added, "and try to keep track of the two junior angels who will be on either side of you."

That's when I broke out in a cold sweat. "Who are they?" I said. "Who was supposed to play this part, anyway? Why didn't she show up?"

"You said you always wanted to be an angel and they wouldn't let you," she said with her blue eyes doing their number on me. "Now's your chance."

SHOW TIME!

I didn't find out who my two fellow angels were until T. R. gave me a shove and I was on stage. As I climbed up onto a teetery stool behind the cardboard stage, two mini-angels mounted their shorter stools on either side of me. The one on the left was swathed in a Barney sheet. He grinned up at me, gums shining where his front teeth should have been. The one on my right was a pink, fluffy-haired blonde with wide, innocent eyes. I was just thinking, *How much trouble can she be?* when her entire costume, constructed from a Sesame Street sheet, slid off her shoulder. Big Bird threatened to crumple to the floor before the makeshift curtain even opened. She lunged for it.

"Don't move up there!" T. R. hissed to her from behind.

The kid froze. At least I wasn't the only one intimidated by T. R. And that was definitely the only reason I found myself standing up there flanked by toothless junior juvenile delinquents. *Talk about lame,* I thought, with the wisdom of age.

But when the curtain yanked open and a sea of oohing and aahing parents was revealed, the actor in me kicked in. I tried to appear angelic as I looked down into the "stable" below me.

Two teenagers were staged there in an assortment of sheets and bathrobes. The girl was holding a bundle of something I assumed was the baby Jesus. *Probably somebody's Cabbage Patch doll,* I decided. Then my attention was diverted to a crowd of shepherds and a rather large herd of livestock who charged up the aisle while the woman at the piano played "O Come All Ye Faithful." Most of the kids sang. One of them—with cow horns made out of toilet paper rolls—mooed.

Not a bad costume, I thought. I wish I'd thought of that seven or eight years ago.

But I had *real* problems to think about right now, and they were on either side of me. The angel on the right was quickly losing control of her costume, and with T. R.'s warning still ringing in her ears, she didn't dare move even as Big Bird slid slowly down her arm. On my left, the other angel said in a voice as loud as the school intercom, "I have to go to the bathroom." I was grateful for the mooing, without which the whole congregation would have heard it.

" 'And they came with haste,' " a narrator said as the final strains of the carol faded.

"Haste" wasn't the word for it. As the kids crammed themselves around the stable, several of the smaller sheep were trampled by the sixth-grade cattle, and one lamb started bawling his eyes out. The toilet paper cow kept mooing.

On my right, Big Bird was hanging precariously from one elbow, and on the left I heard, "I have to go *bad*."

I smiled angelically and hissed to the right, "Grab it with your teeth!" and to the left, "Can you wait five more minutes?" I myself wasn't sure *I* could. This was definitely the most embarrassing thing that had ever happened to me. Here I was, fourteen years old—

And then something else happened.

" 'But Mary kept all these things,' " the narrator said, " 'and pondered them in her heart.' "

SILENCE OF THE SEASON

There was a hush as all eyes turned to the actress below me. It was suddenly obvious, even to the horde of squirming livestock—even to me from my perch above her—that the girl playing Mary was into it. If Marvin Shields had been there with his pen and pad, he'd have given her a rave review.

Even with thirteen-year-old Joseph standing stiffly next to her looking like he'd rather be having a root canal, she bent over the bundled-up doll in her lap, tenderly stroked it, then looked up at the crowd of admirers. One graceful hand came up and beckoned them all in closer. Even I leaned in for a better look.

Good grief, Jill, I thought to myself, *it's just a Cabbage Patch doll!* But I craned my angel head anyway to see more.

The shepherds and cows and sheep and donkeys saw it first, of course, and then the damp-eyed mommies and daddies sitting in the church. I was probably the last to realize as she pulled the blanket from his face that the doll was moving.

His pink, chubby face was puffed up to cry—and with a balling up of his little soft fists, he *did* cry. The doll was a real baby.

All around him the chaos became a portrait of wonder and awe. Fifty pairs of eyes shined. Fifty little mouths rounded into red ohs. Fifty little minds believed they were seeing the baby Jesus. Mine was one of them.

THE MEANING OF CHRISTMAS

Everything was still, even on my left and right, as all us kids were suddenly in Bethlehem, standing under the stars, staring down at a real baby. *This isn't just any baby,* their faces seemed to say. *This baby is important. He's somebody special. This* moment *is special.*

In the midst of the silence, I realized I'd missed my cue. The baby Jesus' face was uncovered, and I was supposed to deliver a line—but I was clueless as to what it was.

"Jill!" T. R. hissed from behind me. "Go!"

"Praise the Lord!" I burst out. "We are all children of Jesus!"

There was a moment of blank looks, and the woman

at the piano peered over her glasses at the script. She finally started in on "Joy to the World," and the kids started chirping. The angel on my left crossed his legs, and Big Bird on my right slithered to the floor.

I grabbed them both, scooping up Big Bird as I went, and the three of us hauled off the stage. T. R. was standing there, ready to shove the toothless one toward one bathroom and the half-naked one toward the other with sheet in hand.

THE TRUTH COMES OUT

When they'd made their exit, she punched me lightly on the arm. "Thanks for helping out," she said.

I shrugged. "It was—it was cool," I said.

Of course, her blue eyes were boring into me, and I figured out she already knew it had been more than cool. She knew I'd seen some *real* faith out there and some real innocence—the kind I'd lost, not just about Christmas but about everything.

I also figured out something else.

"You were supposed to play Gabriel, weren't you?" I said.

She snorted and jabbed a thumb into her chest. "Does this look like an angel's face to you?" she said.

As a matter of fact, it did. It was a don't-mess-with-me face, but the Christ in Christmas was glowing from every pore.

I shrugged again and said, "Well, I gotta jam." I turned to look for my parents so Mom could gurgle over me.

"Hey, Breckenridge," T. R. said from behind me, "aren't you going to lose the sheet?"

"Nah," I said over my shoulder. "I wanna wear it for a while." After all, I'd never gotten to be an angel before.

Nancy N. Rue

Nancy N. Rue of Lebanon, Tennessee, is one of the top writers of Christian stories for young people in America today and is perhaps best known for her Christian Heritage historical fiction series co-published by Focus on the Family and Tyndale House Publishers.

Isabel T. Dingman

THE BELLS DIDN'T RING

Oh no! The alarm had failed to ring! And now she would miss Christmas with her family in Manitoba. The last train had already left, and the roads were impassable because of a snowstorm. If only she could sprout wings and fly! Now that was an idea. Planes were still new in the 1920s, and most people feared risking their lives in those small barnstorming two-seaters. Should she risk it?

*M*ilk bottles rattled outside the apartment door, and Molly stirred sleepily. The covers were slipping off; it must be nearly time to get up—school again—no, that was over for a while, she was in Regina at Anne's place. And the alarm had been set for six because the train left at seven.

She groaned softly. What an unearthly hour for a train to leave! And why did girls have to talk half the night when they slept in the same room? Would there be time for another forty winks? There was a shaft of gray light coming through the window; she might as well look at her watch and see.

The room was cold. She shivered as her feet touched the bare floor, and hunched her shoulders together under the thin night gown. It was hard to see the watch face in the light. . . .

"No, no!" she cried, startled, when her sleep-dimmed eyes made out the figures.

"What's 'at?" murmured Anne drowsily from her bed.

"My watch says 7:30, but it must be wrong—where's that alarm?"

With one bound Anne was out of bed, reached for the clock, turned on the light.

"Yes, it says 7:30 too—oh, my dear, whatever could have happened?" she moaned. "It's set for 6—the pointer is at 'alarm', the clock is going, the winder is— Molly, I'll never forgive myself—the alarm spring isn't wound!"

Molly flung herself on the bed and burst into tears.

"Oh, my lands, and I thought I was so careful," Anne went on mournfully. "But listen, dear—there must be some other way of getting home. Can't you take a train tomorrow?"

"The train to my home town goes only on Tuesdays, Thursdays, and Saturdays," Molly said shakily. "By the time I get there Christmas will be all over—the dinner— the presents—and we've never been separated before—" She buried her face in the pillows.

"Well, could you get a train to some nearby point and drive over—say to Granton?" Anne suggested.

A gleam of hope lit up Molly's doleful face. "Phone the station and see," she begged. "It's just 30 miles from home."

Anne turned from the phone discouraged. "It left at 7:25, and is a Daily except Sunday," she reported. "Not another till Monday. But how about driving all the way? It's only 200 miles, and if you can get a car to go I'll pay the difference between the cost and your train fare, I feel so guilty."

"Have you forgotten the blizzard last night?" Molly sobbed. "I thought my train would never get in. There will be drifts four feet deep over the road, a car couldn't possibly get through, and anyhow it would cost a fortune. Too bad I can't sprout wings and fly," she added bitterly.

"A sail, a sail," Anne cried, slipping into her dressing gown. "Your words, my dear, have given me a bright idea. I'll phone Jimmy."

"It's me," she said a minute later. "Old dear, can planes fly in weather like this? Well, listen. My friend Molly Marstone's here—that teacher from Poplar Creek I told you about—and she's missed her train home because I made a mess of setting the alarm. Her home's at Pike—some little place in Manitoba with the most awful train service, and there won't be another till Tuesday. It's tragedy, I tell you—family of twelve, always together on Christmas, and she has a whole suitcase full of presents tied up in tissue paper, and it'll just about kill her if she doesn't get there. Would one of the airmen take her over and what does it cost?—Fifty dollars? Oh, man, remember she's just a poor school teacher and I'm a working girl myself—What's that? Publicity? Well, I'll say she wouldn't mind! There's not much she wouldn't do to get home. I'll ask her."

Molly was sitting up on the bed, wide-eyed. "What are you talking about?" she asked, twisting her hands nervously.

"It's like this," Anne explained. "Jimmy's a reporter, but on the side he does publicity for the airplane company. They're having a hard time making people believe that flying in winter is safe and pleasant. Now it would cost fifty dollars to charter a plane, but Jimmy says if you'll let your picture go in the papers, with a story about teacher from the frontier flying home to a family reunion and all that, he's sure one of the boys will take you over for nothing! Could anything be more gorgeous?"

"Fly—picture in the paper—Oh, Anne, I couldn't—" Molly began.

"All right, then, if you'd rather miss going home," Anne said, turning to the phone.

"Oh yes, I'll do anything—tell him I will—ask him to let us know about arrangements—Anne, this is terrible," she cried incoherently. This was more like a nightmare than any day before Christmas she had ever known!

She sank back against the pillows, trembling. Fly home to Pike—all that way? Why, she had been scared even to go up at the Exhibition when so many of the girls had taken ten minute flights which supplied them with conversation for weeks. And in winter too—it was terrifying. But if she didn't, there was a dreary week-end, the awful anti-climax of arriving after the great day was over—she might as well risk her life—she'd want to die anyway if she couldn't be home for Christmas. And having her picture in the paper—the trustees and all the people in the school district would talk, and the girls she had been to Normal with—but after all, it was nothing to be ashamed of to fly. Wouldn't the old town be excited, though—they'd arrive before the train, so she wouldn't need to wire the folks. With a sudden upward tilt of her chin Molly began to dress.

Jimmy arrived at 9 o'clock.

"It's O.K." he announced. "Dutch Baker will take her over, and the papers are willing to use the story, with cuts. News is always dead the day before Christmas. They should be pretty snappy pictures too," he added, looking at Molly approvingly. "You're to go to the photographers now and have some shots, then we'll take more at the landing field. Come right along—Dutch is in the car downstairs. You won't get away till nearly noon, as the plane has to be overhauled a bit, but we've got to rush to get those cuts in."

"You're a lucky girl," Molly whispered to Anne as they put on hats and coats. "I'd give my eyeteeth for a beau like him. You should see my swains at Poplar Creek!"

A tall man in aviator's uniform was standing beside Jimmy at the curb. When he turned towards them Molly's heart missed several beats. Those were the bluest eyes she had ever seen. She seemed to be drowned in their blueness—his face was so bronzed, that was why—and he was very erect and held his head like a prince. It could never be true that she was to ride 200 miles in an airplane with him. Pretty soon the alarm would go off—but Jimmy was going through the motions of making introductions.

"So this is the little girl who nearly missed Santa Claus," the god-like person said, in warm, rich tones which sent a series of little shivers up and down her spine. "Well, our bus is guaranteed to overtake any team of reindeer that ever set out from the North Pole. Your worries are over now; sit back and have a good time."

Molly tried to speak, but somehow the words wouldn't come. *He'll think me the dumbest thing that ever came out of the backwoods,* she thought miserably. Unfortunately she could not see how big and bright her eyes were, or what a wild-rose flush had spread over her cheeks.

At the studio, pictures were taken of Molly alone, and Molly beside the airman, and Molly with her arms full of the parcels which would not have had a chance of being Christmas presents but for his aid. Then came instructions about what to wear, a quick change, and more shots beside the plane, with Molly in leather coat, helmet, goggles, and fur-lined boots. A hurried luncheon—and she was climbing, trembling, into her seat, and Dutch was fastening a leather belt around her waist. Anne kissed her hastily, whispered, "He's single, dear—Merry Christmas"; Jimmy shook hands and assured her there was nothing to be afraid of; and with a loud roar the plane left the snow-covered field and soared gracefully into the air.

Oh, such a din! Surely something must be wrong with the engine. Molly clutched the leather strap, and looked anxiously at the pilot. But he seemed perfectly calm. Goodness, she felt queer already—wouldn't it be dreadful if she was airsick. They had stopped going up now, and were heading northeast, towards the obscure little corner of the woods where Pike lay. She plucked up courage to look over the edge, and smiled in spite of her fears to see how absurdly small the streets and houses and people looked. Nobody was paying any attention to them, either—planes were as common as cars now, not like the time she had first seen one at Brandon Fair.

After the first exciting moments, Molly sat back and snuggled down inside the high fur collar, fur robe, and other wrappings. It was comfy—she could almost go to sleep, with that monotonous humming in her ears—but it would be a great waste of time to sleep now. Even if she lived to be a grizzled old maid teacher retiring on her pension she could always get a thrill out of remembering this Christmas Eve ride through the clouds. It wasn't only the new sights and sounds and sensations. It was more being close to the most wonderful man she had ever seen in her life. If only she hadn't been so tongue-tied when she met him or there was some chance now to show him how nice she could be. But it was no use trying to talk above that roar, and as for coquettish glances—Molly chuckled at the idea of a swathed mummy trying to send languishing looks through goggles. If only he would stay and spend Christmas with them! But he intended to start right back after they landed, and make Regina again before dark.

It was one of those perfect winter days which often come on the prairies around Christmas time. Heavy snow had fallen the night before, covering the ugly fields and bare woods with a thick blanket of dazzling whiteness. There was no wind, the sky was a kindly gray, and the air was like wine. The whole country seemed hushed, waiting for the magic of Christmas to spread its sway.

As the miles sped past, however, the sky became darker, a breeze sprang up, and occasionally flakes of snow floated past. Molly noticed that Dutch was intent on his controls, and no longer turned back to wave reassuringly from time to time. Terror gripped her heart. If a blizzard came up, they'd have to stop—there wouldn't be any danger, of course, but they might be stuck in some little dump on the prairie for days before it would be safe to go on. He'd hate her for having got him into it. But oh, if the snow kept away for another half hour they'd be there. Already she recognized the Assiniboine River, and the hills to the south.

Ten miles from Pike, the storm came up in earnest, and the roar of the wind mingled with the roar of the north wind in a duet horrible to hear. But the snow was not too thick yet—the spires of the little town could be seen, and she had explained to Dutch about the fields nearby where it would be safe to land. Just a few minutes would get them there.

She signaled wildly to him, pointing downwards to Brady's pasture field. That was one of the best spots of all, and just half a mile from home. He nodded assent, the nose of the plane turned earthwards, and with a slow, gliding motion the machine started down. They couldn't be more than five feet from the ground now—all danger was over—but what on earth was that crashing sound? One wing of the plane had caught on a barbed wire fence, and while the body landed smoothly on the snow, there was a sickening droop to the canvas spread out so proudly a moment before.

Dutch jumped out and helped Molly to alight. She was so stiff and frightened that she could hardly stand, and had to steady herself by clinging to his arm. "Oh, I'm sorry! Is it really serious?" she asked, pushing back her goggles and looking at him with tear-filled eyes.

"Serious enough, I'm afraid," he answered. "But in any case I couldn't start back till the storm was over. Don't let it spoil your Christmas. Where do we go from here? Will you trust me with that precious suitcase?" And they trudged side by side through the whirling snow.

It was all so different from what she had expected! The town didn't even know they were here—and she felt so badly about this accident—but it had its points, too; he'd have to stay over night anyway, even if he did fly back next day. Still, he likely had a date with some girl in Regina, and would be sore.

"I suppose this is going to upset all your plans for Christmas?" she said sadly.

"Not a bit of it—there ain't no such thing," he said. "I was asked to go to a party tonight, which would likely have lasted till tomorrow afternoon, but I hadn't decided to be there. That kind of a party doesn't seem right for Christmas Eve, somehow—it's one time when I remember the old days at home."

"Haven't you a home now?" the girl asked softly.

"Been alone in the world for the last five years," he said. She did not answer, but her sympathy made the silence warm and vibrant as they walked on through the barrage of snowflakes.

Molly turned in at the gate of a big, rambling house with wreaths of holly in every glowing window. Racing up the steps she threw the door open, and rushed into the living room with a joyous "Yoohoo!" Brothers and sisters of assorted sizes sprang up like Jacks in the box from chairs and sofas, her mother stretched out eager arms, and half-laughing, half-crying, the girl rushed into them, while shrieks and questions and greetings made a deafening noise.

For a moment she forgot all about Dutch—but only for a moment. Then she turned and saw him standing in the background, looking shy, almost wistful! Remorsefully she darted towards him, caught him by the arm, and drew him into the circle, where she introduced him to her family, ranging from wee David, aged four, to married sister Mary who had two babies. Then they sat in front of a roaring fireplace, while the little sisters pulled off Molly's boots, the little brothers took charge of Dutch's helmet and overcoat, and everybody from David up asked questions and tried to tell bits of news.

Oh, she was happy! And she'd have missed it all if it hadn't been for him!

When Dutch got up and said he had better be going to the hotel, there was a storm of protest. In the first place, there was no hotel; and even if there had been, they wouldn't allow him to go there, when he had been so wonderfully kind. The boys especially made it clear that he would depart only over their dead bodies. The aviator had replaced the cowboy, fireman, and engineer as youthful idols, and to have one as a Christmas guest was the height of bliss.

Molly was afraid that he might be bored. But he seemed to be having a good time that evening, with two or three youngsters on his knee and older boys trying to talk to him seriously. He appeared to enjoy the carols, which were a family tradition on Christmas Eve, and joined in lustily. Christmas Day he went to church in the morning and ate enormously at dinner time. And on Monday it took a lot of persuasion from air-minded youths to go to Brady's pasture and see just what was wrong with the plane. Molly was very glad that he hadn't got it fixed before dark. Now he could go with her to the dance in the town hall. Really, her family had been so devoted that she herself had hardly seen anything of him!

It was the same at the dance—all the girls wanted to be introduced, and they were with a party both going to the hall and coming home. But on the morning of December 27, he found her alone in the little upstairs den.

"Busy?" he asked, coming in and sitting down beside her. "I've come to say goodbye—those repairs can't be stretched out any farther with all those sharp-eyed boys looking on."

"Why—what—" she began, with a puzzled frown.

"I couldn't help it," he said. "It would have been very easy to go back Sunday morning, but I had to see more of you. I didn't know there were any girls like you left, or any families like yours. Gee, Molly, what have you done to me? I—"

The door opened and four young brothers came in and gathered around Dutch. He looked at the girl in dismay.

"Listen—we'll never have a minute alone here," he whispered. "Will you come to Regina a day ahead of time when you go back to your school? I've a lot to tell you—and something very important to ask you."

"Meet the train on Friday," she said softly.

"I will," he answered. "And young woman, if you miss this one—"

"I'll go and set the alarm myself, right now," she replied.

Isabel T. Dingman

Isabel T. Dingman wrote during the early part of the twentieth century for family magazines in Canada and the United States.

A ROSE IN WINTER

Her son, John, was gone and no longer believed in God. How could she face the onslaught of the years— alone? And Christmas was the hardest time of all.

But one Christmas morning, there in the snow— was a rose.

CIRCA 1904, VERMONT

Two figures stood silently beside the new grave, not thinking it a strange place to be at almost midnight on Christmas Eve. The tall one, a man with too much gray in his dark hair for being in his early forties, held his treasure gingerly, close to his heart. Indeed, the bouquet of seventeen dried roses had grown old and very fragile with the passing of time. With a slightly trembling hand, he lightly fingered the brittle, paper-like petals of one especially misshapen rose, not surprised when it began to crumble, almost like snow melting, to his gentle touch.

The other figure, stooped with age, watched him quietly. Finally she dared break the pristine silence. "They were her favorite Christmas decorations, you know," she said softly.

"And for too many years," he said, his voice breaking, "her only ones."

"Yes, but somehow they were enough," murmured Rosa, remembering.

Margaret Vincent was not afraid of being alone. She had wrestled with aloneness many times before, always with strength and faith. She knew it and lifted her chin in slight defiance as a young girl when given the whispered title of *orphan* by her schoolmates, coupled with their pitying stares. She faced it bravely because she had to when she buried her two-month-old daughter, Louise, while Thomas was away at war fighting in President Lincoln's Union Army. Yes, she was nearly paralyzed with overwhelming sorrow when less than a year later, in April of 1862, two army officers in crisp blue uniforms knocked at her door, informing her of the loss of her husband in the far-off battle of Shiloh. Still, the people of the village were amazed at how soon she rallied beneath her grief to go on alone. But she wasn't alone, really. There was God. And there was little John.

"John-John," as she affectionately called him, at three was already so much like Thomas when Margaret began the task of parenting alone. Anyone could see, and understand why she lived for, and poured her whole soul into the raising of this mischievous, curly-haired boy. More than just the usual mother-son relationship, they were inseparable friends through the younger years of his growing so that Margaret even began to forget her past losses and grief. The love and the laughter they shared filled the small house by the big, grassy field where the boy spent endless hours of imaginative adventure as a cowboy or a pirate. Often the boy persuaded his mother to join him in his rompings in the field. In turn, he cheerfully accepted her frequent invitations to "help" with her baking and other tasks about the house, though it really meant more labor for her.

Margaret worked hard, and often into the night, as a seamstress to supplement the small army pension she received each month for their living. Still it was a good, satisfying life. They had everything they needed, didn't they? They had each other, didn't they? Yes, she could see a streak of stubbornness in her son as he inched toward the teen years, but wasn't it just that same strong spirit she had so admired in her husband, showing itself in a different cloak?

"Mama, I want to tell you something . . . something very important."

Margaret's needle stopped in mid-air and she looked up at him. "Yes, John-John?"

"That's just it, Mama!" he announced emphatically. "I don't want you to call me John-John anymore. My name is John Thomas Vincent!"

"I know, Son. I named you. Remember?" Margaret said gently.

"Well, yes. But I want to be called just plain 'John.' It sounds . . . well, it sounds more grownup-ly," he said sternly. His ten-year-old shoulders were thrown back in a stance of determination but the one lock of unruly hair that stuck straight up on the left side of his curly head gave him anything but a look of maturity.

Margaret managed to raise her sewing to her face, as if for a closer look, just in time to hide an amused smile. "I see," she said. "Any other reasons?"

"Oh, Mama," he said earnestly, his voice softening, "I don't mean to hurt your feelings. It's just that the other boys tease me when they hear you call me. They even have a song they sing about it!

John-John. Poor widow's son.
There's your Mama. Better run!

John looked down at his scuffed, over-worn shoes. "They say I'm just a 'mama's boy' and that we're very poor."

Setting aside her sewing, Margaret rose wearily from the old chair, all her former amusement gone. She crossed the faded rug in the little room and put both hands on John's shoulders.

"Look at me, Son. We may not have a lot of fancy things, but the Lord has never let us go to bed hungry or into the streets to be cold, has He? We have enough. We have each other and we have our faith."

"But Mama! If God loves us so much like you always say, why did baby Louise die from the measles? And why did my daddy have to die in the war? Why can't I have a father like the other boys?"

Margaret later wondered if she had said the right words in her attempted explanation of God's loving sovereignty and this world's harsh realities. Maybe she should've worded it differently or called for the village pastor to come talk to the boy. Could his questions have been more fully answered, his years of bitterness averted? She would always wonder.

At the end of their talk, she simply put her arms around her son and promised to try to remember to shorten his name to the desired one-word title. His return hug, usually so fiercely enthusiastic it almost hurt, seemed half-hearted and weak.

The small fellow's "pirate and cowboy" years passed and the "other boys," as John called them, became increasingly more important in her son's life. Margaret spent many hours, late into the night, upon her knees praying for God to watch over her fatherless son. She began to question her every decision as a parent, for whatever she did seemed to be the wrong thing in John's eyes. And all the sacrifices she made, taking in more and more sewing, working until her fingers were sore and her eyes could no longer focus, to buy him some of the things the *other boys* had, never seemed enough. *His* eyes that had once been the exact replicas of Thomas', earnest and kind with a sparkle of hidden fun in their gray depths, had grown increasingly hard and cold, almost steely. Yes, they still had some good times together, but they were fewer and fewer between John's moods of quarrelsomeness or stubborn silence.

The one, rare peaceful time that Margaret could always seem to count on came at Christmas. Back when Thomas was alive, they had started the tradition of going as a family to the midnight candlelight service in the village church on Christmas Eve. After his death, Margaret no longer felt she could take her small son alone out into the dark, snowy night. So she had begun their own Christmas Eve candlelight service at home, reasoning that allowing her delighted youngster to stay up very late one night a year couldn't hurt him that much.

Every year it had been the same. Just before midnight, she would light the candles on either side of their simple wooden nativity, the one Thomas had carefully carved by hand. Next she and John-John would bow their heads to thank God for sending the gift of His Son, Jesus, to be their Savior. Then they would join hands and sing "Silent Night," John-John's warbly little boy voice join-ing Margaret's sweet soprano. Afterward would follow their traditional treat, warm gingerbread and milk, before Margaret scooted a still wide-awake little lad off to his feather bed.

Margaret smiled as she remembered all those precious early days. Where had they gone? She longed to walk

down the hall *this* Christmas morning and peek in on
that tiny, sleeping boy . . . to playfully tousle the little
head of dark, curly hair. To see a bright, eager smile on
his young face and eyes that still reflected his father's
character would be her best gift.

Instead, she dreaded the thought of waking him. Last
night, at their Christmas Eve candlelight time, John had
seemed subdued, but not sullen. When they had joined
hands to pray, he had bowed his head respectfully and
at the end of the prayer, he seemed to hold her hand a
little tighter, a little longer than usual. As she began to
sing "Silent Night," after a few measures he had softly
joined in, his young-man voice breaking awkwardly
on the notes now and then. It had gone rather well,
Margaret concluded.

But how would he be this morning? Back to the
same sullen, easily-angered seventeen-year-old who
refused to experience the common joys of life all around
him? Would he insist on leaving right away to be with
the "others" in their wild holiday revelry?

Slowly, hesitantly, and praying for wisdom as she
walked, Margaret headed to John's room and opened
the door quietly.

"Good morning, Son, it's time to get up."

Crossing the room to his rumpled bed, she spoke a
little louder.

"Merry Christmas, John! Time to open your packages!
I think you'll like what I . . ."

She stopped in mid-sentence, her heart beating
wildly. Trembling, she pulled back the layers of hand-
made quilts to reveal three pillows, placed to look like

the shape of a sleeping person. On one of them was a
short note. A note, but no John.

With tears blurring her vision, Margaret could barely
make out the hastily scrawled words:

> Dear Mama,
>
> Please understand. I had to go. I just don't believe
> like you do anymore. I don't want to hurt you but
> I must live my own life. Don't look for me. I am
> going far away. I do love you.
>
> Your son,
>
> John

Margaret was no stranger to grief and she was a
woman of strength and faith. *But this! This* was aloneness as she had never known it. Her anguished cries
echoed eerily across the snowy field where John-John
had once played.

Rosa stood, hands on her ample hips, surveying her
garden. This summer's would be better than the last, she
was sure. And look at the roses! They were literally singing with color and life in their soft, full clusters. What a
beautiful bouquet they would make! Impulsively, she
reached her hand into the pocket of her dirty gardening
apron and pulled out the pruning shears.

The sun was shining brightly and perspiration began
to make little beads on her plump face as Rosa crossed
the field between the two small cottages. She didn't

know quite what she was going to say to Margaret Vincent but it was high time she said something. Maybe her roses would do the talking.

Everyone in the small village had certainly done *their* share of talking . . . gossip it was, and Rosa said so to those who tried to explain to her the neighbor boy's disappearance last Christmas. Her no-nonsense glare and plain rebuke had caused them to turn to others with their low-spoken, behind-the-hand guesses as to why the boy had run away. But she was well aware of Margaret's pain and withdrawal, just the same.

She and Margaret, though neighbors by way of the big field, had never really been close friends, but they had always spoken cordially in the market and chatted after church services. Before John left, Margaret's life had seemed complete and happy with the raising of her son, and Rosa always found plenty to occupy her time in the comings and goings of her own grown children and grandchildren. Now Rosa saw that her neighbor ventured from her home only upon complete necessity. True, she still came to worship, but she averted her eyes and hurried past the hands of those who would reach out to her. Not rudely, but as one moving quickly away to protect a wound from further injury.

Well, the wound was not healing on its own, Rosa surmised, as she walked purposefully up to the front of the house whose shades were drawn sadly, even on this sunny day. Taking a deep breath, she knocked firmly on the weathered door.

Slowly, tentatively the door opened slightly. Margaret peered out cautiously, yet almost eagerly, as if she were somehow hoping to see someone else standing there.

Disappointed though not unkind eyes looked at Rosa.

"Hello, Margaret. May I come in?"

"Umm . . . yes. Yes, of course," Margaret stammered, remembering her manners just in time to prevent embarrassment for them both.

Rosa noted how pale and thin the already slightly built woman had become in the past few months. She took in the slumped shoulders that looked as if they had borne for too long, a weight no one should bear alone.

"I brought you these," Rosa said, thrusting forth the fragrant bouquet.

"Roses!" Margaret cried, her face almost lighting with their beauty. "Rosa . . . these flowers . . . how did you . . . well, how could you know they were my favorite?" Her eyes suddenly had a faraway look to them as she murmured softly, ". . . a message . . . an errand for God."

"Message?" Rosa queried.

Margaret came to herself and motioned Rosa towards the old wing-backed chair. "Won't you sit down? Let me put these in water and . . ." she turned hesitantly to her friend, ". . . if you like . . . I mean, if you have the time . . . I'll tell you about it."

"Oh yes, please tell me, dear!"

Rosa sat down and sighed with relief, glad that she had come after all. Her friend hadn't resented this intrusion into her private grief. She needed to talk.

And talk she did. After months of silence, and before that, those years of only short, labored conversations with her angry son, the pent up words seemed to spill out of Margaret's heart as she told Rosa about the roses' message.

Years ago, she explained, shortly after Thomas was killed in the war, Margaret had begun to sink into a dark depression which even her cheerful little boy could not break. No one in the village knew about it because she was able to stay at home most of the time, but it was there all the same. The tallied losses of her life just seemed too great and her strength to cope, too little. One day, as John-John was outside playing, she fell on her knees beside her bed, asking God for some sign of hope for the days ahead, some ray of beauty to penetrate her gray world, a reassurance that He really knew and really cared. How could she go on without the love of her Thomas? Even in her woeful praying that day, she had stopped to remember his sweet ways.

When she had become acquainted with this young man, the handsome but quiet Thomas Vincent, for the first time in her life, Margaret no longer felt like a forgotten, unwanted orphan. As long as she lived, she would never forget the warm summer evening he had shown up at the front door of her boarding house wearing a shy but hopeful expression on his face and carrying a dozen red roses for her.

He had always treated her with such respect and affection, continuing to court her, even after they were married. He even brought her flowers from time to time. Sure, they were just wildflowers he picked beside the lane on his way home from work, not the roses he had once brought her before they married. But who could afford roses for a young family in those days?

How she did love roses though! She had even carried a small bouquet of them on her wedding day. And now with Thomas gone, would she ever receive flowers from anyone again? Did even *God* know that the void of being, once again, alone and uncared for threatened to destroy her sanity? All these painfully sweet memories and troubled thoughts had stormed in parallel turbulence through her mind along with her desperate prayers that day.

Just at that moment, Margaret continued to Rosa, little four-year-old John-John had entered the house and walked into her room, holding something furtively behind his back.

"Mama, I picked dese for you. Dey were in dah woods 'cwoss dah field." Then he had looked at her with those big, Thomas-like eyes and lisped, "Am I in twouble?" With that, he pulled forth a grimy little hand, clutching a trio of small wild roses, their stems broken raggedly. John-John knew he wasn't supposed to venture beyond the fenceless boundaries of their yard, and he had especially been warned never to go alone into the dense, dark woods that bordered one side of the field.

With her voice breaking, Margaret went on to tell her friend how she had wildly hugged her little fellow, explaining to him that, no, he wasn't in trouble. He had run an errand for God to help make Mama happy again. She had let him know that his scraggly bouquet of roses had been a message of hope to her, a message that she was still loved and watched over affectionately. Of course, she had gently but firmly warned him not to go into the woods again without her permission until he got much older.

Turning to Rosa, she started to say something more, then stopped, putting her face in her hands. A painful moment of silence passed.

"Oh, Rosa! I feel like he's in the dark woods again. Only this time, he's far away where I can't reach him. He doubts the very existence of God, and I'm not sure he knows how very much I love him. I guess . . . I've failed . . . failed completely as a mother."

At this, Rosa, who, contrary to her frank, talkative nature, had only sat quietly listening, nodding her head affirmatively now and then as the distraught mother talked, broke in.

"No, Margaret. You're wrong about that. Everyone in the village knows you have been a most wonderful mother. And John knew that too. Why, I once saw him lick one of those bullies who was mocking and calling you 'the poor widow woman.' That John! You should've heard him! He said it right out loud to the big ruffian. He said you were 'the best mother ever and if anyone else called you "poor" they would answer to him!' I was there, Margaret. I heard him! A failure? Nothing could be farther from the truth!" Rosa was never one to mince words.

Margaret lifted her lined face from her hands and turned swollen eyes upon Rosa's kind countenance. "Well, I don't know . . . but anyway, thank you, my friend, for the roses. You, too, were on an errand for God. And somehow, I still believe John will come home . . . to God and to me someday."

The two ladies talked deeply for another hour. Margaret told Rosa about the little Christmas Eve tradition that she and John used to share, along with other sweet memories of the past, as if in the telling, they would return. Finally the elder woman went her way, vowing to remember. The younger, holding the vase of roses close to her face and breathing in their fragrance, though still heavy in heart, watched her go, glad that she had come.

Could a year already have passed? Margaret wondered as the day began. Tonight would be her first Christmas Eve without John. How, she wondered, does one truly celebrate the birth of Christ while trying vainly to tend a shattered heart? How could she sort the good remembrances, which she so desperately needed to hold dear at this time of year, from the one awful memory of that moment when she pulled back the quilts to discover John was gone? She had no idea how she would get through the next two days.

Across the field, Rosa, too, was up early to begin her preparations for the day. As she pulled ingredients out of the cupboards to start baking, she remembered her vow. She would not forget her friend.

Later that afternoon, Rosa knocked at the door of Margaret's house. With a large platter of baked goods, too large for one small woman to consume but there all the same, she announced a hearty "Merry Christmas, Margaret!"

"Oh, Rosa! Thank you. All this for me? I . . . well, I baked nothing this year," her eyes darted around the plain room, "and I couldn't make myself decorate the house either. Except for putting up the nativity, of course." She forced a brave smile. "I guess I needed to at least see the reminder that He is Immanuel . . . God with us." She sighed softly, almost to herself. Then looking back down at the heavily laden tray she brightened. "Won't you come in?"

"I'd love to, dear. But I have to be on my way. Lots more to do yet before the children and grandchildren arrive." And with that, Rosa bustled, as quickly as her round frame would allow, back across the snowy field. She had vowed; tonight she would remember.

At midnight, more out of habit and duty than joyful devotion, somehow Margaret lit the candles on either side of the crèche and bowed her head to thank God for sending His Son.

"And Father," she continued, "wherever my son is tonight, let him know that Your Son loves him and can give him what his heart truly seeks. Keep John safe, and if it be Your will, bring him home to me again. In Christ's name, amen."

She lifted her head, but when she tried to lift her voice to sing "Silent Night," tears, not words, came. Quietly, she blew out the candles and went to bed.

On Christmas morning, Margaret opened the front door to get a few more sticks of wood for the fire when she saw something lying on the step. It was in bright contrast to the stark, white snow that lay beyond in the yard: a single, red rose. Under its petals lay a piece of simple stationery, folded in half with these two words written on it: *Keep believing.*

Margaret tenderly held the rose to her heart and looked across the field to where her friend lived. That Rosa! A rose in winter, no less! She saw the tracks in the snow leading across the field and marveled at the trouble the woman would have to go to in making such a delivery. First, she would have to send away to the big city for the rose. There were no fancy florists with hothouses in their tiny village. And the expense! Rosa was not a wealthy woman, Margaret knew. And then to traipse across the slippery field at night . . . why, she could've fallen and broken her neck! It was chore enough for the short-legged, heavyset woman in the day time! Margaret would have to talk to her.

The chance to thank her friend and mildly scold her for going to such trouble did not come till well after the new year. A heavy snowstorm hit the day after Christmas, keeping all but the heartiest of souls inside for nearly two weeks.

When Margaret finally saw Rosa at a much-needed trip to the village market for both of them, she began to thank her friend for the special gift.

"Oh, Rosa! How I've been wanting to see you! I can't tell you what your gift meant to me on Christmas Eve. But such extravagance and trouble . . ."

"I won't hear a word of it. It was in my heart to do since the day we talked last summer. Say no more."

When Margaret started to protest again, Rosa, always the blunt one, exclaimed, "Enough! You have shopping to do, my friend, and the weather looks threatening again. Not another word." With a quick hug, the women parted.

Back at home, Margaret hung the still fresh rose upside down to dry. She wanted to save this new message of hope from God. She would need to see it again, she was sure.

And so began a new tradition. Every Christmas Eve,

Rosa would come in the afternoon with her tray of baked goods. And every Christmas morning, Margaret would find a rose on her door step. Under the rose would be the note with the same message: *Keep believing*. Each Christmas, Margaret would bring out the dried roses from the years before and set them in a vase on one side of the nativity, next to the candle. On Christmas morning, she would put the fresh rose in another water-filled vase on the other side. There was no ornamented tree, no wreath, no garland, no mistletoe or holly berries in her little cottage. The roses were her only Christmas decorations.

Would it really be five years now? Five years of looking out the window, watching for a tall young man to come striding briskly across the field. Five years of listening for a husky voice to say, "Mama, I'm home!" And five years of a rose in winter, along with the encouraging messages to keep believing, just when she needed them most.

Margaret's thoughts turned to her faithful neighbor, Rosa. How her name fit her! She had been like the roses, a very message of hope to her lonely friend. At the same time, Margaret's conscience smote her. Rosa's great giving certainly hadn't been returned in kind. So consumed had she been with her own loss, that Margaret's usually generous nature had eroded to only the sending of a heartfelt note of thanks to Rosa for her nighttime walks across the field and her roses in winter. And Margaret's notes had been only slightly more wordy than Rosa's. They said simply: *Thank you for the gift and the hope. Love, Margaret.*

But tonight would be different, Margaret vowed. Tonight, she would bake the gingerbread she had not baked for years, not since John had left. And she would stay awake to catch her friend when she left the rose, insisting that she come in by the fire to have the warm gingerbread and perhaps a cup of tea. It was high time she thought of someone beside herself, she chided inwardly.

Margaret could scarcely suppress a laugh as she met Rosa at the door that afternoon. She graciously accepted the baked goods, offering the invitation to come inside that she knew by now would be refused with a merry smile by her neighbor who must scurry on her way.

"But you'll come in for sure tonight, my rosy friend!" Margaret chuckled to herself as she closed the door. "I'll see to that!"

Humming to herself, Margaret wondered at the stirring in her heart tonight. But then, her pleasures had been so few, for so long, that even the meagerest delight seemed a festival to her joy-starved spirit. Midnight was approaching and it would soon be time to light the candles. The gingerbread was cooling on the sideboard and its spicy fragrance filled the air. Such anticipation she felt at being able to surprise her friend with this little act of kindness! She had even sewn a small present to give to Rosa. It was a beautiful scarf of lovely, warm material. On its corner she had embroidered a delicate rose. Margaret was known throughout the village for her fine needle work and she knew her friend, though a plain, practical person, would be delighted with the gift.

Nervous with expectancy, she adjusted the dried roses, four of them, in their vase beside the nativity. She had kept them in a special, tissue paper-lined box all year long and they were still in wonderful condition, despite being fragile.

Suddenly the clock chimed twelve times. Margaret lit the candles and stood in the warm light of their soft glow before the nativity. With head bowed, she thanked God whole-heartedly for the gift of His Son, and for the gift of her friend, Rosa. And she thanked Him that those who were lost to her, her parents, Thomas, little Louise, and now John, were not lost to Him.

Opening her eyes, she began to sing for the first time in years.

Softly at first . . . "Silent night, holy night."

Then louder with more joy than she could've believed possible . . . "All is calm, all is bright. Round 'yon virgin mother and child. Holy infant so tender and mild. Sleep in heavenly peace, sleep in . . ."

Wait! Was that a noise she heard on the steps? Yes, she heard it again. It was Rosa! She had to catch her before she scurried back across the field.

Flinging the door open, Margaret saw the rose on the step. She hurriedly picked it up and glanced at the note in her hand. Two words. Almost the same . . . yet different.

The note said simply: *I believe.* Margaret stood puzzled at this new message.

Looking up, she saw the shadow of a figure cast by the bright moonlight upon the snowy yard near the corner of the house. *Rosa must have been standing there for a while, watching me, and now she's hiding, trying to sneak away,* Margaret realized. But . . . such a tall, thin shadow on such a short, round woman? Her whole body gave a start and she nearly dropped the rose.

"John?" she called in a teary whisper, almost fearing to believe what she knew in her heart to be true.

Then louder, "John? Is that you, Son?"

The figure stepped out into the full moonlight now. He was taller, and broader as he strode toward her, his pace quickening with every step, but she knew her son.

"Mama! . . . Mama!" he cried. He was running now.

"Mama, I'm home!" He held her in his strong arms, the rose crushed between them. "Oh, Mama!" he repeated again and again.

For a long time they stood there, till his convulsing sides stopped heaving and she pulled him gently inside the warm house. They sat in the candlelight near the nativity and talked until all the wax had melted and Margaret had to light the lantern. Then Margaret, ever the mother even in such times, cut the gingerbread and poured the milk, which John devoured in huge bites between their sweet communion.

He told of the far-off land, the *dark woods* as she would ever think of it, of his years of wandering. Sparing only the worst details which he could not bring himself to inflict upon her, he spoke of his bitterness at life and his unbelief in a God who would take away the loved ones of a woman as good as his mother, leaving a little boy fatherless. He admitted his foolishness in choosing companions that would further destroy his faith and introduce him to pleasures of the dark side of life.

As he looked into the thin, wan face of his mother, almost haggard yet glowing with love, he grieved at how she had aged in the past five years and earnestly begged her forgiveness.

"Oh, John. I forgave you years ago. Your return tonight is the greatest gift of my life! But I have to ask you, Son, about the roses? And the notes? Were they all from you?"

"Yes, Mama."

"But how? I thought . . ."

John shifted uneasily in his chair. "Mama, that first year, I just wandered anywhere, tramping all across the country. I filled my heart with so many things that I was able to keep pushing you out of my thoughts. But when it came close to Christmas, I began to hop trains, heading for home. I had to see for myself that you were all right. And as I came through the last city before our village, for some reason I remembered the time I gave you the wild roses when I was a little boy and how they had made you happy. So I used the last of my money to get a rose to bring to you.

"I brought a little stationery with me, intending to write you a simple note, telling you that I was fine and not to worry. But, as I stood watching you from outside the window that first Christmas Eve after I had run away, I wondered if . . . if you still believed. I wondered if you would still light the candles and pray when you had lost so much. If you didn't, I knew I could justify my own unbelief in a God who would allow so much unfairness in the world.

"But as it got closer to midnight, I suddenly realized that, though *I* didn't believe, I still wanted *you* to keep believing. You were my only candle in the darkness, the only ray of hope I had that . . . that God is good and love is real."

Turning his eyes to the frosty window, John continued. "I held my breath and waited out in the cold. And sure enough, at midnight, you lit the candles and prayed. I waited to hear you sing . . . but you didn't."

John paused and looked down at the soft, but workworn hands of his mother which he held in his own big hands. When he spoke again, it was with a tremor of remorse in his voice. "And then I knew *I* was the one who had stolen your song. The other boys at school used to call you the 'poor widow woman,' but I was the only one who had made you poor. I can't tell you how ashamed I was at that moment.

"So I wrote those words, put them under the rose and left, going back across the field in the same tracks I had seen and walked in earlier. And each year, no matter where I found myself and in whatever condition, I had to come home at Christmas to see if you still believed."

A tiny stream of liquid joy slipped down Margaret's face. She was filled with an immeasurable gladness that she had prayed when she least felt like praying. Now she waited quietly for the rest of John's story that she knew was coming.

He took a deep breath, as if to inhale some of the abundant goodness that was all around in this home, *his* home, before continuing. "Then tonight, as I was watching you, all at once I just knew that everything you had taught me as a boy is true. Not just in spite of, but *because of* all your hardships and losses, as well as mine, it made sense to believe that a loving God would send His Son to a world like ours to be the Savior.

"And Mama, when you started singing again, I could hear the true joy in your voice . . . so I wrote, 'I believe.' I was going to leave the rose and the message and head back to the city for a couple of days. I've been working and saving up a little money and there's something I need to do there. But then you stopped singing and came outside. I tried to hide in the shadows but you saw me. And . . . oh, Mama," his voice broke as he looked into her face, "it's just so good to be home, really home, again!"

There, thought Margaret, *there are those eyes of Thomas again.*

The sunrise was painting its glorious hues of pinks and violets and golds which reflected back from the snowy field the next morning, Christmas Day, as Margaret crossed it with her present to give to Rosa. Her surprised friend listened with joy to the news of John's homecoming and Margaret's story of the roses.

"So you see," Margaret concluded, "I thought it was you who brought me the rose every Christmas Eve. Of course you know," she hastened to add, "I've always been so grateful for the wonderful baked things. I've had no other form of feasting on the holidays, but your tray of kindness."

Rosa smiled warmly at her friend. "Not to worry, my dear. The mistake is understandable. When you told me in the market, that first time, how extravagant my gift was, I thought you meant the size of the tray that I brought you." She chuckled in remembering. "It was an awful lot of food for one small lady. And I wouldn't let you explain.

"However, the breads and cookies and cakes were

not my only gift to you." Rosa went on in a voice smaller than was normal for her. "The other was given in secret.

"You see, that summer day when I first brought you the roses and you told me your troubles, I vowed to spend every Christmas Eve at midnight on my knees, praying for the safe return of your boy. The Father heard me in secret and has rewarded me openly. I, too, have received two gifts this Christmas. The first, your beautiful rose scarf. The second, the gift of answered prayer." The two friends embraced in a tearful hug of triumph; the kind that only victorious soldiers can share after a hard-fought, and finally won battle.

John soon returned from the city, bringing his mother a son who was new on the inside, one who would stay and believe, and a dozen red roses. Of course, she dried the roses and each year put the large, fragile bouquet beside the nativity. And every December, though the little cottage was adorned, once again, with a decorated tree, fragrant evergreen wreaths, lots of garland, holly berries and mistletoe, the roses remained Margaret's favorite decorations through their many Christmases together.

❋ ❋ ❋

The two stood a moment more looking at the new gravestone. Would her heart have given out on her while she was still a relatively young woman in her early sixties, if she hadn't known those awful years of grief and aloneness? John would always wonder. His eyes traced the words carved beneath his mother's name and the date of her birth and death. They had been her last to him before she closed her tired but peaceful eyes in death, to be reunited with her parents and Father and little Louise in the presence of Jesus: "Keep believing." Beneath that, John had added: "Blessed is she that believed: for there shall be a performance of those things which were told her from the Lord. Luke 1:45"

"Silent night . . ." Rosa began to sing in her quivering, old voice. The soft, loose folds of her ancient throat were covered warmly by a rose-embroidered scarf.

"Holy night . . ." John joined in, bending to tenderly lay the roses on his mother's grave.

Jodi Detrick

Jodi Detrick, pastor's wife, director of dramatic productions, and mother of three teenagers, lives in and writes from Chehalis, Washington. She is a prolific writer, whose work is published in magazines such as *Christian Reader, Today's Northwest Woman,* and *Pentecostal Evangel.*

Frederick William Roe

AN ILL WIND

---

*It was the day before Christmas, and tempers were
frayed. The heat was stifling. Then a window was
yanked up, and a sudden wind blew a blizzard of
paper who knows where. Alas for poor Tommy: That
all-important check the boss had entrusted to him was
gone! So, too, most likely, was his future with the
company.*

*In order to get this story into perspective, keep in
mind the fact that, adjusting for inflation, one dollar
when this story was written would equate to about
fifteen today.*

A telephone call for Mr. Wharton!" called the telephone clerk, turning from her instrument.

The *slap, slap, slap!* of a wide paste brush on paper, which had been vying with the endless clicking of typewriters in the busy office, ceased abruptly as the paper hanger left his table to answer the call. At the same instant the rasping of a buzzer beneath Tommy Reynolds's desk caused that young man to rise quickly and disappear through a door marked Private into the manager's office.

"Who turned on that steam again?" demanded an irritated feminine voice in the main office. "It's hot enough in here to boil anyone alive. And the smell of that paste—ugh!"

"Of course the boss had to have it done the day before Christmas, when everyone is tired and mad and busy!" a girl at an adjoining desk exclaimed. "There weren't enough people and things to fall over without having a paper hanger around!"

"Perhaps," another girl suggested mildly, "the boss thinks it won't do for Crane and Company to have that big smoke spot on the wall any longer than is absolutely necessary."

Miss Babcock, the first speaker, was not to be soothed. "Well, *I'm* going to open a window and get some fresh air!"

Inside the manager's office Mr. Gregory was giving Tommy Reynolds his instructions. "Go right over to the bank with this check," he said as he wrote his name across the back of the paper.

Taking the check, Tommy hastened into the outer office. He paused at his desk, slipped one corner of the check under the rubber foot of a wire basket filled with orders, and began to put on his overcoat. At that moment Miss Babcock proceeded to gratify her desire for fresh air by flinging up a window near by. A tremendous blast of cold winter air rushed into the room. Wild confusion reigned among the employees of the office near the open window. The air filled abruptly with fluttering papers and wildly grabbing hands.

"Put it down!"

"Shut the window, somebody!"

Tommy's flat-top desk was nearest the window and suffered most of all. His order basket, piled high, contributed a fluttering deluge of sailing papers, which, as Miss Babcock closed the offending window with an impatient bang, settled slowly to the floor.

The paper hanger, returning from the telephone, found himself just in time to prevent his freshly pasted strip of wall paper, aided by the sudden breeze, from slipping to the floor. Since it was all ready to go on the wall, he deftly caught it and, slapping it against the plas-tered surface, quickly brushed and tapped it into place.

With his coat half on, Tommy Reynolds whirled about; his first thought was of the check caught by one corner under the wire order basket. It was gone! Flinging off his coat, he joined the rest in picking up papers from the floor. When he had gathered all he could find he placed the loose pile on top of his desk and searched them hurriedly. A quick glance at the wall clock showed that it was quarter of three o'clock. If he were to get to the bank before it closed, he had not a moment to lose.

He went through the pile of papers twice, but the

missing check was not among them. Again he searched the floor; he examined the contents of the wastebasket and he even dragged his heavy desk from its position to see whether the check could have blown under it. A second glance at the clock showed him that it was eleven minutes of three. The situation was becoming desperate. Tomorrow would be Christmas—and the next day, Sunday. Whatever Mr. Gregory's reason for wishing the check cashed immediately, it would soon be too late to get it cashed before Monday morning of the following week.

Tommy hastily appealed to his fellow employees, and they joined him in a search of other desks, piles of papers and wastebaskets; but their efforts were fruitless. By this time it was so late that it was useless to think of reaching the bank before the doors closed.

Tommy told Miss Greene, the cashier, of his predicament. "I'll have to go in and tell Mr. Gregory about it before long," he said with a groan.

"It's too bad, Tommy," she replied. "Although it wasn't your fault altogether, yet it *was* careless of you to let a check get out of your hands even for an instant, especially after it had been endorsed and *anyone* could cash it. I happen to know all about that check. It came in the mail this afternoon from a man who has been owing us a bill for a long time. When the check came Mr. Gregory was a little suspicious and called up the bank. They told him he had better get it cashed immediately, before the account was overdrawn. So you see why he wanted to get it in this afternoon.

"Still," Miss Greene went on, "if it's cashed the first thing Monday morning, it can't make so *very* much difference. But—you *must* find it. If you shouldn't, Mr. Gregory would have to stop payment on it at the bank and write Mr. Giltner for another, and the chances are that that gentleman would take advantage of our carelessness in losing it and refuse to send it again. And the firm would be out $98.61. Now go and tell Mr. Gregory just how it is—the sooner you have it over with the better."

Sick with apprehension, Tommy knocked at the manager's door. Fortunately, Mr. Gregory was alone.

"Mr. Gregory," Tommy said, plunging at once into his confession, "I slipped a corner of that check under my wire order basket for a minute while I put on my coat to go to the bank. Miss Babcock opened the window next to my desk, and the wind blew papers all over the floor. That check blew away with the rest, and I've looked everywhere for it, and I can't find it."

"You haven't been to the bank yet, and you've lost that check!" cried the manager. "You don't mean to tell me—" The big man stopped abruptly and sat staring straight ahead of him. The sudden silence was ominous. Trembling from head to foot, Tommy stood waiting. The subdued confusion of the outside office was hardly noticeable above the ticking of the little desk clock as it measured the seconds into minutes.

"Go find that check, and don't come in here again till you do!" said Mr. Gregory suddenly.

Tommy turned, fled through the door and collapsed into the chair at his desk.

There was much—very much—work to be finished before the holiday, and Tommy realized that until that was done he must postpone further search for the check.

Sick through and through with apprehension and despair, he forced himself to bend to his tasks. An hour of hard work steadied him somewhat. By supper time he had regained his equilibrium.

On this last day—the last night even—of the holiday rush, Tommy knew he could expect little help or sympathy from any of the other dozen employees round him. For the last month the night work had been growing heavier. Beginning with eight o'clock, the hour for stopping had gradually grown later, until during the last week midnight had been reached—and passed—by some of the office force.

As Tommy returned from a hasty supper and the busy evening wore on, it became apparent that the small hours of the morning would come before the last of the weary toilers should depart for home. Mr. Gregory was always among the last to leave; none worked harder than he. At midnight the light still shone steady and bright from his office.

Late that afternoon, in accordance with his usual custom, Mr. Gregory had given to Miss Greene for distribution among his employees a small pile of envelopes. In each envelope was a short personal note commending the recipient for faithful service during the past year and wishing him, or her, a Merry Christmas and a Happy New Year; there was also in each envelope a gift of money proportionate to the employee's position in the office. There was no envelope for Tommy this year—a fact that further increased his misery.

As the hour grew late and one after another of the office force finished work and left for home with a cheery "Merry Christmas!" Tommy's spirits sank lower and lower. Soon everyone would be gone, and his weary, hopeless search for that missing check must begin. Christmas indeed! It was already Christmas, he grimly reflected as he glanced at the clock. The hands were exactly together at five minutes past one.

A little later Tommy noticed with a slight start that the office was deserted. Except for Miss Greene and Mr. Gregory, everyone else had gone. Even as he glanced toward the cashier's office the light above her desk went out, the wire door snapped shut, and Miss Greene crossed the outer office to Tommy's desk.

"Tommy," she said, drawing up a chair, "I know just how you feel. You're discouraged, you feel like throwing up your job with the firm, and you think Mr. Gregory's a hard boss. But now put yourself for a minute in his place. He's been working late every night for the last two months, harder than any of us. Then Clancy set a wastebasket afire, nearly made a panic in the office and smoked the wall all up, and now *you* go and lose a bad-account check that he's been after for months.

"Now I'm going to tell you something that not another soul in the office except Mr. Gregory knows. I wasn't going to tell you for fear it would discourage you, but I think maybe it will help you instead. Robert, the young fellow who used to have your job, was a great joker and tease. One afternoon about half past two he was waiting outside the cash window while I finished counting out a pile of bills that he was to take to the bank. The last bill happened to be a new, crisp one-hundred-dollar note.

" 'Whew!' Robert exclaimed when he saw it. 'You're not going to faint at the sight of so much money, are you, Miss Greene? Allow me to give you a little fresh air.'

"And before I knew what he was doing he had grabbed an electric fan and switched on the current so that the sudden blast of air came across the shelf and almost directly into my face. That hundred-dollar bill went right up into the air. Robert said it sailed clear to the wall at the back end of my cage and then shot down toward the floor. I brought both hands down on top of the remaining bills and kept them from scattering.

"I was too thoroughly annoyed and exasperated to speak a word. It was dark near the floor at the back end of my cage, and I couldn't find the missing bill. Robert offered to help me, but I was irritated and wouldn't let him. Instead, I sent him off to the bank with the rest of the money while I locked my cage door and searched every nook and cranny for that bill.

"At the end of half an hour I had to give it up. It was as if the floor had opened and swallowed it up. When Robert returned from the bank and learned that I couldn't find it he was scared, for he knew that it was his thoughtlessness that had done the mischief. The next morning he failed to appear for work, and we have never seen or heard of him since.

"Well, Mr. Gregory was very kind and exonerated me of all blame, but I felt that next to Robert I was responsible for losing that bill, and I made it up to the firm. It's two years now since that happened, and I had almost forgotten all about it, but your losing that check today brought it all back."

"That's the reason Mr. Gregory stopped calling me

down all of a sudden after I'd told him about the check this afternoon!" Tommy exclaimed.

"Of course it was," replied Miss Greene. "He was thinking of Robert. Now, I don't want you to make the mistake that Robert made. Whether you find that check or not, you stick."

"Miss Greene, you've helped me a great deal, and I want you to know I appreciate it. It's when a fellow is down and nobody seems to care that it's hard."

"Yes, I know," said Miss Greene softly.

For a few moments after Miss Greene had gone, Tommy sat with his head sunk into his hands. He was very tired. He'd far rather go home and sleep than look for a lost check. The sudden roll and rattle of Mr. Gregory's desk top as it closed roused him. The door of the manager's office opened, and Mr. Gregory came out.

"Well, my boy, how are you coming on? Found that check yet?"

"No, sir, I haven't," Tommy replied. "I've only just finished my other work; but I'm going to find it if it's in this office."

"That's the talk. Go after it—now, while there's nobody round to bother you. Report to me the first thing Monday morning how you come out. Good night."

"Good night, sir," answered Tommy as the door closed behind his employer.

He was alone. Only the slow, measured tick of the big wall clock broke the silence. How different that ticking was from the nerve-racking sound of the busy day! Turning on all the lights, Tommy began his search. He rolled every desk aside from its place to bare the floor beneath, then put them back again; he searched thoroughly through every wastebasket. Finally, he entered Miss Greene's cage—she had thoughtfully left the wire door unlocked for him—and with a movable electric light began to peer between the tubes of the radiators from end to end, and behind and underneath them.

As he rose from inspecting the last radiator he heaved a sigh of disappointment. There was only one other place in the whole office worth investigating, and that was under and behind the letter-file cabinet that stood against the wall just outside Miss Greene's wire cage.

Of course there were other possibilities: the check might have fluttered out the window or fallen without being noticed into one of the few desk drawers that were now locked; or some one might have instantly recognized its value and, amid the temporary confusion, stolen it; but those possibilities seemed too remote to Tommy to be worth considering seriously, and he turned his attention to the filing cabinet.

The big case was heavy, but by moving each end out alternately a little at a time he managed to hitch it as far as its own thickness from the wall. The dust of years lay thick on the floor and hung from the brown wall paper behind it.

"Good chance to do a little cleaning up, anyhow!" Tommy muttered.

He got the office broom and dustpan and set to work to sweep up the dirt. Suddenly the wooden baseboard separated from the plastered wall behind with a startling *crack!* The sharp sound attracted Tommy's attention, and upon looking closer he saw that on either side of the filing cabinet the board had long been warped. With a thrill he wondered whether the lost check could have slipped down in the narrow space between the baseboard and the wall.

Steam heat from the radiators is what warped the board, he said to himself as he looked round for some thin, flat instrument with which to explore the narrow space.

The steel ink scratchers and the letter openers were all too short; the rulers were too thick. At last Tommy cut a long strip of stiff pasteboard, which served the purpose admirably. Beginning near the corner of the room where the crack started, he pushed the piece of pasteboard along the crack toward the filing cabinet.

Presently he struck some object, and, with his heart pounding fast, worked to bring it into view; but it proved to be only an old stamped envelope, and with an exclamation of disgust he cast it aside.

Continuing his search, he reached the wire partition that separated the cashier's office from the outer office.

Might as well make a good job of it while I'm at it, he said to himself.

He got up from the floor and, going round to the inner office, continued his investigation of the crack. He had scarcely advanced three feet when his strip of pasteboard again encountered some obstruction. The next instant Tommy brought the object into view. For a moment he stared at it with widening eyes; then he pulled it from the crack.

In his hands he held, still crisp and stiff—*Miss Greene's long-lost hundred-dollar bill!*

As Tommy rose to his feet a little selfish choke of self-pity came into his throat. Miss Greene would have a happy Christmas now. Then, with a sudden impetuous rush, a fierce, startling temptation assailed him. No one could possibly ever know! He could make good the lost check, probably keep his position, and even get some pity from his fellow employees—from Miss Greene at least. Pity from Miss Greene! After *stealing* a hundred dollars from her! Why, she was the best friend he had! She had tried her best to hearten him when things had looked black and hopeless. And he was thinking of *stealing* a hundred-dollar bill that she probably needed a great deal more than he needed it!

"Finding is keeping!" he muttered. But not when you know who the owner is. And anyhow—what kind of a fellow am I?

The struggle was over. Tommy hurried to his desk and scribbled a note:

My dear Miss Greene,

Merry Christmas! I found this bill at the back end of your office in a crack behind the baseboard.

Tommy

He enclosed the note and the bill in an envelope, which, after he had sealed and addressed it, he placed securely in the inner pocket of his coat. Then he returned to his task of probing the remaining length of crack in the cashier's office. He quickly finished it, tried the board upon the other three sides of the other office, which yielded nothing, and finally brought up at Clancy's desk, where he slumped wearily into the chair.

Dropping his chin into his hands, he stared moodily at the wide panel of fresh paper that the paper hanger had so recently put on the wall between the big windows.

"Mr. Gregory doesn't *mean* to be harsh. Why couldn't Clancy have waited till after Christmas to set his old wastebasket afire? That plain paper is too light-colored, but I suppose—"

His jumbled reflections ceased abruptly. His eyes suddenly narrowed and concentrated themselves on a dark-brown rectangular outline on the buff-colored wall in front of him. Silently, with a swift leap of uncertain hope, he drew out his pocket knife, strode over to the wall and with three quick strokes slit down one side and across the top and the bottom of the dark, damp spot. Bending back the flap of paper that he had cut from the wall, he tried with trembling thumbs to separate its edge into two pieces. For a moment he thought that he held indeed only one thickness between his fingers; but presently it yielded, and he slowly peeled from the still damp inner surface of the wall paper—*the missing check!* It was somewhat blurred, but otherwise unharmed.

Pressing back the flap of paper against the wall, Tommy smoothed it firmly into place until the three slits were scarcely noticeable. Then, placing the check beneath a blotter and a heavy weight, he sat down for a moment to let it dry out and to recover from his excitement. He glanced up at the clock. The hands showed half past two. As he was speculating on the extraordinary place in which he had discovered the lost check, the telephone rang with sudden, startling clearness in the silent office. To his astonishment it was Mr. Gregory's heavy voice that came over the wire.

"Is that you, Tommy?" it asked.

"Yes, sir," answered Tommy.

"How are you coming on? Found it yet?"

"Yes, sir, I have."

"Thought you would. Where was it?"

"Under a strip of wall paper that the paper hanger put on this—I mean yesterday afternoon. It must have blown over and stuck face down on a fresh-pasted strip of paper, and he put it on the wall without seeing the check. I happened to notice the dark spot on the wall where the paste wet through the paper. But, *Mr. Gregory,* I found something else! I found that hundred-dollar bill that Miss Greene lost two years ago. It was down in a crack between the baseboard and the wall at the back end of her office. And I'm going to give her a Merry Christmas with it tomorrow."

Mr. Gregory's voice seemed suddenly to grow deeper over the wire as he replied:

"Well, Tommy, if Miss Babcock hadn't opened the window and the wind hadn't blown in and—well, you know the old proverb, 'It's an ill wind that blows nobody good.' You get right home now, quick, and go to bed. And Tommy—listen. Before you leave, go into my office and raise the top to my desk—it's unlocked— and you'll find an envelope there for you—your envelope! Good-by and Merry Christmas to you!"

Frederick William Roe

Frederick William Roe wrote for magazines such as *The Youth's Companion* during the first quarter of the twentieth century. Today little is known of him.

Judith Wade

CARLA'S CHRISTMAS GIFT

_They were braving the rickety steps because they were
worried about "that Polish kid." When they arrived,
they could see that things were not going well at all._

_This was not going to be a good Christmas for
either Carla or her overworked mother._

*W*ind howled through the hall of the shabby frame house as Beth Duncan and I climbed the rickety stairs to the third floor. Both of us were half frozen. Beth said, "I never thought I'd climb that many steps for anybody. But this Polish kid has me worried."

Carla Grabowsky had been in our class only since summer, but all of us liked the quiet, golden-haired girl with her quaint accent. The fact that she had been absent for two Sundays disturbed us.

I think one thing which had won our hearts was that Carla and her mother were so utterly alone in the world. She had told me once that they had come from Poland when she was a baby. Her father had been forced to leave by enemies who had political power, and the family had escaped to the coast, intending to sail for America. Passage could only be secured on separate ships because of the crowds then leaving Europe. Carla and her mother had reached this country, but her father had been arrested as he was about to sail. That was the last they ever heard from him. Carla's mother had given up all hope, knowing what all too often happened to those who were arrested under those circumstances. They had drifted to the vicinity of Boston where the mother worked in a factory to support the two of them.

Beth and I stopped to catch our breath and decide on which of the four doors we should knock. Beth said, "This must be it. It's the only clean one." So we knocked and waited.

We heard something moving stealthily inside. Then the door opened a crack and a blue eye peered out. The next moment the door opened wide and Carla was standing there smiling. But the smile faded as she said with some embarrassment, "I thought it was the land-lord. He's coming for the rent—and we're not ready. He gets mean when we're late paying him."

From inside the room a woman spoke in Polish. Her voice sounded thin and tired. Carla said, "Mother would like you to come in and have some coffee."

We followed her inside. I saw a frail, gray-haired woman in a rocking chair by the window. She seemed old. Then I realized it was not years but her slight figure and weary eyes that gave the appearance of age. Carla said, "Mother, this is our teacher, Miss Wade, and Beth Duncan."

We sat down and Carla brought cups and a big pot of coffee. Beth said, "Carla, we missed you in class. Our Christmas party comes next Friday, and we're expecting you to sing that Polish song in costume, as you promised!"

The night of the party finally came, and the assembly room was filled. Our church is in a downtown area where many foreigners live, and a number of them had agreed to sing their folk songs that night. Behind the curtain there were a lot of colorful costumes, and every-one was excited.

Then Carla arrived. She had her peasant dress in a paper package, but there was no sparkle in her blue eyes. She seemed close to tears. I asked her what happened.

She hesitated a moment, then said, "Remember the day you were at our house? The landlord came after you left. He threatened to put us out if we didn't pay. That's why I wasn't sure I'd be here tonight. It took every cent we had, even what I had saved to buy a

Christmas gift for my mother. I'd saved it nickel by nickel from what I'd earned taking care of a little girl whose mother works in a defense plant. Now—I'll have no gift for Mother."

I said, "Don't worry, Carla. We'll find a Christmas gift." I knew our class would meet this emergency. But Carla wasn't cheered. Just then the first number was announced and she hurried away to put on her peasant dress.

I went out into the audience. The program moved smoothly and everyone seemed enthusiastic about it. Finally Carla's song was announced.

People stared, then applauded, as she appeared. She wore a short black skirt and a quaint bodice.

There was a plaintive note in her young voice as she sang that song from far off Poland where brave men are still fighting for the freedom they love and refuse to surrender. Then a strange thing happened.

A man came slowly down the aisle. He was tall and well dressed. He sat down in the front row of chairs, but his eyes never left the face of the girl.

As she finished, and while the crowd applauded, he started toward the door which led to the room behind the platform. I met him there as Carla came out into the assembly room. But he paid no attention to me. He said abruptly to Carla, "What is your name? Tell me! Who are you?" His voice was intense, and he spoke with an accent.

Carla was frightened, and I stepped to her side. When he saw me, he said, "I am sorry. But—that song. I have not heard it for years. Then, as I was passing this church tonight, I heard a child's voice singing this song which my father wrote. He was a musician, as I am. I used to sing that song to my little daughter. I did not know anyone else knew it."

Carla was staring at him now. So was I. I said, "This is Carla Grabowsky. She is a Polish girl in my Sunday-school class."

"Grabowsky!" he said. "The name means nothing. But this child—she is the image of my wife who came to America years ago from Poland. I was to follow her—but was detained. When I came, I could not find her, though I searched everywhere. Last week I came to Boston to play on a radio program which is sent by short wave to Poland. I am a violinist. My name is Casimir Carlasky." He took a card from his pocket to verify his statement.

Carla's eyes had not left his. She seemed to be in a dream, as she said softly, "Carlasky! That is our name. Grabowsky is the name my mother took here in America. She was afraid to use our own. But she always called me Carla—it's part of my own real name."

I saw the man's face light up. He said, "And your mother's name? It is Marya, is it not?" Carla's eyes went wide in surprise.

His hand reached out and touched Carla's soft hair. Then he drew her into his arms, as he said gently, "After all these years of searching—I have found my little daughter. Take me to your mother, child; she will know me!"

"You—are my father!" Carla said wonderingly. "You must be. My father's name was Casimir. I have heard my mother say it. Come. We will go to her." After that she dissolved into a stream of Polish and we didn't know what she was saying.

The blue eyes were shining. And as the two of them turned toward the door, Carla said, "Oh, Miss Wade, we did find a Christmas gift for Mother, didn't we!"

Judith Wade

Judith Wade wrote for Christian magazines during the second quarter of the twentieth century.

O. Henry

BULGER'S FRIENDS

It was the winter of 1892, and times were hard in the South. Ice and snow came on unrelentingly, and money was scarce. Finally, as contributions dried up, even the Salvation Army admitted defeat: No Christmas tree this year!

So it was that Bulger, the beater of the big bass drum, left the Salvation Army headquarters and went out into the night.

*J*t was rare sport for a certain element in the town when old Bulger joined the Salvation Army. Bulger was the town's odd "character": a shiftless, eccentric old man, and a natural foe to social conventions. He lived on the bank of a brook that bisected the town, in a wonderful hut of his own contriving, made of scrap lumber, clapboards, pieces of tin, canvas and corrugated iron.

The most adventurous boys circled Bulger's residence at a respectful distance. He was intolerant of visitors, and repelled the curious with belligerent and gruff inhospitality. In return, the report was current that he was of unsound mind, something of a wizard, and a miser with a vast amount of gold buried in or near his hut. The old man worked at odd jobs, such as weeding gardens and white-washing; and he collected old bones, scrap metal and bottles from alleys and yards.

One rainy night when the Salvation Army was holding a slenderly attended meeting in its hall, Bulger had appeared and asked permission to join the ranks. The sergeant in command of the post welcomed the old man with that cheerful lack of prejudice that distinguishes the peaceful militants of his order.

Bulger was at once assigned to the position of bass drummer, to his evident, although grimly expressed, joy. Possibly the sergeant, who had the success of his command at heart, perceived that it would be no mean token of successful warfare to have the new recruit thus prominently displayed, representing, as he did, if not a brand from the burning, at least a well-charred and sap-dried chunk.

So every night, when the Army marched from its quarter to the street corner where open-air services were held, Bulger stumbled along with his bass drum behind the sergeant and the corporal, who played "Sweet By and By" and "Only an Armor-bearer" in unison upon their cornets. And never before in that town was a bass drum so loudly whacked. Bulger managed to keep time with the cornets upon his instrument, but his feet were always woefully unrhythmic. He shuffled and staggered and rocked from side to side like a bear.

Truly, he was not pleasing to the sight. He was a bent, ungainly old man, with a face screwed to one side and wrinkled like a dry prune. The red shirt, which proclaimed his enlistment into the ranks, was a misfit, being the outer husk of a leviathan corporal who had died some time before. This garment hung upon Bulger in folds. His old brown cap was always pulled down over one eye. These and his wobbling gait gave him the appearance of some great simian, captured and imperfectly educated in pedestrian and musical maneuvers.

The thoughtless boys and undeveloped men who gathered about the street services of the Army badgered Bulger incessantly. They called upon him to give oral testimony to his conversion, and criticized the technique and style of his drum performance. But the old man paid no attention whatever to their jeers. He rarely spoke to any one except when, on coming and going, he gruffly saluted his comrades.

The sergeant had met many odd characters, and knew how to study them. He allowed the recruit to have his own silent way for a time. Every evening Bulger appeared at the hall, marched up the street with the squad and back again. Then he would place his drum in the corner where it belonged, and sit upon the last bench in the rear until the hall meeting was concluded.

But one night the sergeant followed the old man outside, and laid his hand upon his shoulder. "Comrade," he said, "is it well with you?"

"Not yet, sergeant," said Bulger. "I'm only tryin'. I'm glad you would take a man in if he come to Him late like—kind of a last resort, you know? Say a man who'd lost everything—home and property and friends and health. Wouldn't it look mean to wait till then and try to come?"

"Bless His name—no!" said the sergeant. "Come ye that are heavy laden; that's what He says. The poorer, the more miserable, the more unfortunate—the greater His love and forgiveness."

"Yes, I'm poor," said Bulger. "Awful poor and miserable. You know when I can think best, sergeant? It's when I'm beatin' the drum. Other times there's a kind of muddled roarin' in my head. The drum seems to kind o' soothe and calm it. There's a thing I'm tryin' to study out, but I ain't made it yet."

"Do you pray, comrade?" asked the sergeant.

"No, I don't," said Bulger. "What'd be the use? I know where the hitch is. Don't it say somewhere for a man to give up his own family or friends and serve the Lord?"

"If they stand in his way; not otherwise."

"I've got no family," continued the old man, "nor no friends—but one. And that one is what's driven me to ruin."

126

"Free yourself!" cried the sergeant. "He is no friend, but an enemy who stands between you and salvation."

"No," answered Bulger, emphatically, "no enemy. The best friend I ever had."

"But you say he's driven you to ruin!"

The old man chuckled dryly. "And keeps me in rags and livin' on scraps and sleepin' like a dog in a patched-up kennel. And yet I never had a better friend. You don't understand, sergeant. You lose all your friends but the best one, and then you'll know how to hold on to the last one."

"Do you drink, comrade?" asked the sergeant.

"Not a drop in twenty years," Bulger replied. The sergeant was puzzled.

"If this friend stands between you and your soul's peace, give him up," was all he could find to say.

"I can't—now," said the old man, dropping into a fretful whine. "But you just let me keep on beating the drum, sergeant, and maybe I will some time. I'm a tryin'. Sometimes I come so near thinkin' it out that a dozen more licks on the drum would settle it. I get mighty nigh to the point, and then I have to quit. You'll give me more time, won't you, sergeant?"

"All you want, and God bless you, comrade. Pound away until you hit the right note."

Afterward the sergeant would often call to Bulger: "Time, comrade? Knocked that friend of yours out yet?" The answer was always unsatisfactory.

One night at a street corner the sergeant prayed loudly that a certain struggling comrade might be parted from an enemy who was leading him astray under the guise of friendship. Bulger, in sudden and plainly evident alarm, immediately turned his drum over to a fellow volunteer, and shuffled rapidly away down the street. The next night he was back again at his post, without any explanation of his strange behavior.

The sergeant wondered what it all meant, and took occasion to question the old man more closely regarding the influence that was retarding the peace his soul seemed to crave. But Bulger carefully avoided particularizing.

"It's my own fight," he said. "I've got to think it out myself. Nobody else don't understand."

The winter of 1892 was a memorable one in the South. The cold was almost unprecedented, and snow fell many inches deep where it had rarely whitened the ground before. Much suffering resulted among the poor, who had not anticipated the rigorous season. The little squad of Salvationists found more distress than they could relieve.

Charity in that town, while swift and liberal, lacked organization. Want, in that balmy and productive climate, existed only in sporadic cases, and these were nearly always quietly relieved by generous neighbors. But when some sudden disastrous onslaught of the elements—storm, fire, or flood—occurred, the impoverished sufferers were often too slowly aided because system was lacking, and because charity was called upon too seldom to become a habit. At such times the Salvation Army was very useful. Its soldiers went down into alleys and byways to rescue those who, unused to extreme want, had never learned to beg.

At the end of three weeks of hard freezing a level
foot of snow fell. Hunger and cold struck the improvi-
dent, and a hundred women, children and old men
were gathered into the Army's quarters to be warmed
and fed. Each day the blue-uniformed soldiers slipped
in and out of the stores and offices of the town, gather-
ing pennies and dimes and quarters to buy food for the
starving. And in and out of private houses the Salvationists went with baskets of food and clothing, while day
by day the mercury still crouched among the tens and
twenties.

Alas! Business, that scapegoat, was dull. The dimes
and quarters came more reluctantly from tills that jingled
not when they were opened. Yet in the big hall of the
Army the stove was kept red-hot, and upon the long
table, set in the rear, could always be found at least
coffee and bread and cheese. The sergeant and his squad
fought valiantly. At last the money on hand was all
gone, and the daily collections were diminished to a
variable sum, inadequate to the needs of the dependents
of the Army.

Christmas was near at hand. There were fifty children
in the hall, and many more outside, to whom that season
brought no joy beyond what was brought by the Army.
None of these little pensioners had thus far lacked necessary comforts, and they had already begun to chatter of
the tree—that one bright vision in the sober monotony of
the year. Never since the Army first came had it failed to
provide a tree and gifts for the children.

The sergeant was troubled. He knew that an
announcement of "no tree" would grieve the hearts
under those thin cotton dresses and ragged jackets more

than would stress of storm or scanty diet; and yet there was not money enough to meet the daily demands for food and fuel.

On the night of December 20 the sergeant decided to announce that there could be no Christmas tree; it seemed unfair to allow the waxing anticipation of the children to reach too great a height.

The evening was colder, and the still deep snow was made deeper by another heavy fall, swept upon the wings of a fierce and shrill-voiced northern gale. The sergeant, with sodden boots and reddened countenance, entered the hall at nightfall, and removed his threadbare overcoat. Soon afterward the rest of the faithful squad drifted in, the women heavily shawled, the men stamping their snow-crusted feet loudly upon the steep stairs. After the slender supper of cold meat, beans, bread, and coffee had been finished, all joined in a short service of song and prayer, according to their daily habit.

Far back in the shadow sat Bulger. For weeks his ears had been deprived of that aid to thought, the booming of the big bass drum. His wrinkled face wore an expression of gloomy perplexity. The Army had been too busy for the regular services and parades. The silent drum, the banners and the cornets were stored in a little room at the top of the stairway.

Bulger came to the hall every night and ate supper with the others. In such weather work of the kind that the old man usually did was not to be had, and he was bidden to share the benefits conferred upon the other unfortunates. He always left early, and it was surmised that he passed the nights in his patchwork hut, that structure being waterproof and weather-tight beyond the promise of its outward appearance. Of late the sergeant had had no time to bestow upon the old man.

At seven o'clock the sergeant stood up and rapped upon the table with a lump of coal. When the room became still he began his talk, that rambled off into a halting discourse quite unlike his usual positive and direct speeches. The children had gathered about their friend in a ragged, wriggling and wide-awake circle. Most of them had seen that fresh, ruddy countenance of his emerge, at the twelve-stroke of a night of splendor, from the whiskered mask of a magnificent Santa Claus. They knew now that he was going to speak of the Christmas tree.

They tiptoed and listened, flushed with a hopeful and eager awe. The sergeant saw it, frowned, and swallowed hard. Continuing, he planted the sting of disappointment in each expectant little bosom, and watched the light fade from their eyes.

There was to be no tree. Renunciation was no new thing to them; they had been born to it. Still, a few little ones in whom hope died hard sobbed aloud, and wan, wretched mothers tried to hush and console them. A kind of voiceless wail went among them, scarcely a protest, rather the ghost of a lament for the childhood's pleasures they had never known. The sergeant sat down and figured cheerlessly with the stump of a pencil upon the blank border of a newspaper.

Bulger rose and shuffled out of the room without ceremony, as was his custom. He was heard fumbling in the little room in the hallway, and suddenly a thunderous roar broke out, filling the whole building with its booming din. The sergeant started, and then laughed as if his nerves welcomed the diversion.

"It's only Comrade Bulger," said he, "doing a little thinking in his own quiet way."

The norther rattled the windows and shrieked around the corners. The sergeant heaped more coal into the stove. The increase of that cutting wind bore the cold promise of days, perhaps weeks, of hard times to come. The children were slowly recovering the sad philosophy out of which the deceptive hope of one bright day had enticed them. The women were arranging things for the night; preparing to draw the long curtain across the width of the hall, separating the children's quarters and theirs from those of the men.

About eight o'clock the sergeant had seen that all was shipshape, and was wrapping his woolen comforter around his neck, ready for his cold journey homeward, when footsteps were heard upon the stairway. The door opened, and Bulger came in covered with snow like Santa Claus, and as red of face, but otherwise much unlike the jolly Christmas saint.

The old man shambled down the hall to where the sergeant stood, drew a wet, earth-soiled bag from under his coat, and laid it upon the table. "Open it," he said, and motioned to the sergeant.

The cheery official obeyed with an indulgent smile. He seized the bottom of the bag, turned it up, and stood, with his smile turned to a gape of amazement, gazing at a heap of gold and silver coins that rolled upon the table.

"Count it," said Bulger.

The jingling of the money and wonder at its source had produced a profound silence in the room. For a time nothing could be heard but the howling of the wind and the chink of the coins as the sergeant slowly laid them in little separate piles.

"Six hundred," said the sergeant, and stopped to clear his throat, "Six hundred and twenty-three dollars and eighty-five cents!"

"Eighty," said Bulger. "Mistake of five cents. I've thought it out at last, sergeant, and I've give up that friend I told you about. That's him—dollars and cents. The boys was right when they said I was a miser. Take it, sergeant, and spend it the best way for them that needs it, not forgettin' a tree for the young'uns, and—"

"Hallelujah!" cried the sergeant.

"And a new bass drum," concluded Bulger.

And then the sergeant made another speech.

William Sydney Porter
1862–1910

O. Henry was the pseudonym of William Sydney Porter who was born and raised in Greensboro, North Carolina. However, his fame came as a result of the short stories he wrote for the four million citizens of New York City. He is a master of the twist ending and probably the most famous short-story writer America has ever known.

Marian Jeppson Walker

THE TOWN THAT GAVE US JOY

It was a bleak Christmas in the Alberta prairie town of Hillspring, and nothing had gone right for the Jeppson family—had not for a long time. And now, worst of all, the Christmas box from the home folks had failed to arrive in time.

It was enough to break a heart.

Since Family Circle *first ran this story in 1997 it has continued to gain popularity. A number of people have sent me copies, urging me to include it in an upcoming collection.*

*J*t was Christmas Eve, 1927, in the remote prairie town of Hillspring, Alberta, Canada. Mary Thomas Jeppson was getting her six small children ready for bed. She thought her heart would break as she watched five of her children dance around the small house, excited to hang their socks for Santa to fill.

Her oldest daughter, Ellen, sat subdued and sullen in a corner of the cold two-room house. Ellen's heart was heavy for a 10-year-old, but she understood the reality of what tomorrow would bring. She felt that her mother was cruel to let the children get their hopes up when she knew very well there would be nothing to fill the socks. They would be lucky to have a little mush for breakfast as there was only a small amount of wheat and corn left. The winter had just started and already it was cold and harsh. The milk cow had died the week before from starvation and severe weather conditions, and the last two or three chickens had stopped laying eggs about a month before.

Mary helped each one of the children hang a little darned and mended sock. She tried to persuade Ellen to hang one too, but she just sat there, shaking her head and mumbling, "Mom, don't do this. Don't pretend." After the socks had been hung, Mary read the Christmas story from the Bible and then recited a few Christmas poems from memory—and memories of her own happy childhood living in the United States flooded her mind. She was the next to youngest of a very large and loving family. Her mother and father, although they'd been pioneers in a remote area of Idaho, had made life—and especially Christmas—very exciting and memorable.

Before Ellen went to bed, she pleaded again with her

mother to tell the children the truth. Mary kissed her daughter goodnight and whispered, "I can't, Ellen. Don't ask me why—I just can't tell them." It was almost midnight and the other children had been asleep for hours, and Mary's husband, Leland, had gone to bed too, feeling like a broken man, like he had failed his family completely. Mary sat by the fire reading the Christmas story from the Bible over and over again. Her mind drifted to her plight here in this godforsaken land of ice and snow. It was the beginning of the Depression, and her husband had heard wondrous stories about the unlimited opportunities of homesteading in Canada. After two years of not being able to find work in the United States and after a flood had destroyed their small home in Willard, Utah, he had decided to move his family to Canada. It seemed, however, that they were five or six years too late to cash in on the rumored possibilities. After several seasons of unusual weather conditions, most of their crops had frozen or failed.

In October Mary had received a letter from her family back in Idaho, asking what they could do to help and what they could send the family for Christmas. Mary had put off her response—she had too much pride to let them know how destitute her family was. Finally, in November, realizing that things were not going to get any better, she had written. She only mentioned the necessities: she told them how desperately they needed food, especially wheat, yeast, flour and corn-meal. She related how long it had been since she had been able to bake a cake or cookies because they had no molasses or honey and, of course, no sugar.

It had been a year since they had had any salt to use on their food. She also added that it would be wonderful if they could ship just a little bit of coal, because of the cold, and because their fuel supply was almost depleted. She continued her letter with a request for some old, used quilts. All of hers had worn thin and were full of holes, and it was difficult keeping the children warm. She mentioned their need for anything to keep them warm—any used socks, shoes or gloves, warm hats or coats. And at the very end of the letter she wrote, "If you could just find a dress that someone has outgrown that I could make over to fit Ellen, please send that too. Ellen is such a little old lady for such a young girl. She carries the worries of the whole family on her thin shoulders. She has only one dress that she wears all the time, and it is patched and faded. She has outgrown it, and I would like so very much to fix up something that is nicer for her."

Starting the week before Christmas, Leland hitched up the horse and sleigh and made the three-hour round-trip from Hillspring into the town of Cardston every day to check at the train station and post office to see if a package had come from Mary's family in Idaho. Each day he received the same disappointing answer. Finally on Christmas Eve day, he went into Cardston first thing in the morning and eagerly waited for the mail delivery. He left in the early afternoon to get home before dark, and he left empty-handed. He wept openly as he rode home, knowing he would have to explain to Mary that perhaps the package would arrive the day after Christmas or next week, but that it had not made it in time for the big day.

Mary suddenly awoke from her reminiscent sleep with a
chill. The old clock on the wall said it was 3:30 A.M. The
fire in the stove was all but out, and she decided to add
a little more fuel so that it wouldn't take so long to start
in the morning. She looked over at the little limp socks
still hanging by the fireplace and felt a similar emptiness
in her heart. Outside, the wind was blowing at about
70 miles per hour as the snowstorm had intensified.

She was about to put out the lantern and go to bed
for a few short hours when she heard a quiet knock at
the door. Mary went over and opened the door to find
a man standing there, and in all her life she had never
seen anyone look more like her vision of Santa Claus.
He was covered with ice and snow and had a long
beard, made white from the snow. His hat, his gloves
and boots were also white, and for a moment Mary
thought she was dreaming.

It was the mailman from Cardston, who had known
the plight of the Jeppson family. He told her that he
knew they had been waiting for a package from Idaho,
and he knew there would be no Christmas without it.
That evening, as he was finishing up a long day of
delivering mail all around town, he had been glad to be
going home. His horse was exhausted and frozen as that
day had been one of the worst blizzards of the year. He
was relieved to put his horse in the barn, park his sleigh
and return to the warmth of Christmas Eve at home
with his family. But just as he was leaving, someone
from the train station came running up to him and told
him that 10 large crates had just arrived from the States
for the Jeppson family. It was only about 4 in the afternoon, but already it was dark and the storm was getting

worse. They both decided there was nothing they could do about delivering the crates that night, but they would be sure the Jeppsons received them the day after Christmas.

The mailman told Mary that when he went home, he had a disturbing feeling, and after discussing it with his wife, they decided that he needed to deliver the crates that night. He would have to find someone who would let him borrow a fresh horse and a sleigh with sharp running blades. After he finished telling Mary about his decision to come, he brought the crates into the house. She insisted that he thaw out and warm up by the stove while she went out to check on his horse. When she looked at the poor animal with icicles hanging from its nose and mouth, she knew it would never make the trip back to Cardston that night and she tried to talk the man into staying until morning. He refused the offer, telling her that it had taken him almost eight hours to make the journey to her house in the storm, and if he were to leave now, he would still be able to spend Christmas afternoon with his family. So Mary told him she would harness up their own horse, which was in better condition to make the trip back. She got him some dry clothes, fed him what warm food she could muster, and he headed off to town. It was almost 5 A.M. and he probably wouldn't get home until around noon. She thanked him the best she could, but for her whole life she maintained that there would never be sufficient words to express her gratitude. "After all," she would say, "how do you thank a miracle . . . and a Christmas miracle at that?"

As soon as he left, Mary began to unpack the crates. She had only an hour or so before the children would awaken. At the top of one of the crates she found a letter from her sisters. As she began to read the incredible account, tears streamed down her face. They told her that quilting bees had been held all over the Malad Valley, and from these, six thick, warm, beautiful quilts were included. They told her of the many women who had sewn shirts for the boys and dresses for the girls, and of others who had knitted the warm gloves and hats. The donation of socks and shoes had come from people from miles around. The local church had held a bazaar to raise the money to buy new coats and scarves for the whole family. All of the sisters, nieces and cousins, aunts and uncles had gathered to bake the breads and make the candy. There was even a crate half full of beef that had been cured and packed so that it could be shipped, along with two or three slabs of bacon and two hams. At the close of the letter it said, "We hope you have a Merry Christmas and thank you so much for making our Christmas the best one we've ever had!"

When Mary's family awoke that Christmas morning, they awoke to bacon sizzling on the stove and the smell of hot cinnamon muffins coming from the little oven. There were bottles of syrup and jars of jam, and canned fruit that the younger children had never even seen before. Every sock that was hanging was stuffed with homemade taffy, fudge, divinity and dried fruit of every kind. The children didn't even know the names of some of the cookies and goodies that lay before them. Later Mary and Leland were to find tucked in each of the stockings that had been sent for them a few dollars, with a note that the money was to be used to buy coal and fuel for the rest of the winter, and for oats and wheat to feed the animals.

For each boy there was a bag of marbles, and each girl had a little rag doll made just for her. But the most wonderful moment of the whole day was when Ellen awoke, the last to get up, and walked over to the spot where she had refused to hang her sock the night before. She rubbed her eyes in disbelief as she saw hanging there a beautiful red Christmas dress, trimmed with white and green satin ribbons. Ellen turned around, walked back to her bed and lay down, thinking she was dreaming. After her little sisters pounced on her with laughter and excitement, she came back again to the celebration and joy of the most wonderful Christmas ever. For that morning, along with the aroma of good food, the love of a good family, and a new red dress, a childhood had been given back to a young girl—a childhood of hopes and dreams, of Santa Claus, and of the wonder of Christmas.

I will never forget the retelling of this story by my mother, Mary Thomas Jeppson. Although it was always an emotional drain for her to tell it, it was an inspiration to all those who were privileged to hear her story every Christmas since that magical day in 1927.

Marian Jeppson Walker
Marian Jeppson Walker writes from South Jordan, Utah.

Grace Livingston Hill

THE FORGOTTEN
FRIEND

---

*Gordon Pierce had spent generously on himself and
generously on others, but where was an equally
generous Christmas gift for the most important friend
of all? It was a long battle, and it was not won until,
in his mirror, he saw—not one, but two faces.*

*T*he night was inky black and growing colder. Occasional dashes of rain brought a chill as it touched the faces of the hurrying pedestrians. The pavements gleamed black where the electric lights struck them, like children's slates just washed.

Gordon Pierce drew down his hat, turned up his collar, and dropped his umbrella a little lower to breast the gale; but just as he turned the corner into Church Street the uncertain wind caught the frail structure and twisted it inside out as if it had been a child's toy, and the hail pounded down Church Street, rebounding from the stone steps of the church on the corner with such vengeance that the young man was fain to take refuge for the moment in the inviting open doorway till he could right himself or the severity of the storm should pass.

Hail storms are so unexpected that one cannot anticipate them. This one lasted longer than was usual and pelted most unmercifully in at the doorway so that the refugee stepped further into the lighted entrance way of the church, taking off his hat to shake the hail stones from its brim. As he did so his ear caught the sweet strains of the pipe organ within, and a rich tenor voice floated out faintly through the closed leather swinging doors from the lighted room above.

Gordon Pierce was fond of music and knew a fine voice when he heard it. This one attracted him. He stepped nearer and listened a moment, then stealthily pushed open the noiseless door and stepped inside the audience room.

There were only a few people in the brightly lighted church and they were gathered up toward the front near

the pulpit and the choir gallery. The stranger stepped
softly in and stood with hat in hand listening to the
sweet music, then drawn irresistibly he moved silently a
little further down the aisle to a seat somewhat behind
the audience and sat down.

A prayer followed. Until then he had thought this a
small private rehearsal for a favored few. Of course he
could not go out during a prayer, and he bowed his
head in annoyance that he had cornered himself in a
religious meeting by coming so far forward, when he
was extremely anxious to hasten home.

He was meditating a quiet flight as soon as the prayer
should be over, when the same sweet voice that had first
lured him in, broke the stillness that followed the peti-
tion. And this time it was a hymn that was sung. Yet the
voice was insistent, clear, demanding attention.

> *I gave my life for thee,*
> *My precious blood I shed*
> *That thou might'st ransomed be*
> *And quickened from the dead.*
> *I gave my life for thee,*
> *What hast thou given for me?*

The words were so old, but to the young man they
sounded new. It was as if the question had been asked
of his own startled heart by an angel. He forgot about
trying to slip out before the meeting went further on
and listened.

The quiet-faced man who stepped to the edge of
the platform as the singer ceased, and began to talk in
a low but impressive voice, was a missionary, but the

unexpected listener did not know it. He would have been amazed beyond measure if he had known at that moment that he was to be enthralled with interest in a missionary meeting, but this was the case. It was not like any missionary meeting he had ever heard of before though, and he did not recognize it as such even after it was over and he had dropped the last fifty-cent piece his pockets contained into the collection basket with a feeling of annoyance that he had no more.

He had heard things that evening that stirred him deeply.

The storm had ceased when he picked his way out into the slippery streets now white with a fine sleet it had left as a parting salute. As he made his way thoughtfully to his boarding house his mind was still intent upon the new thoughts the speaker had left with him, but when he turned the lights on in his own room he saw a pile of paper parcels and boxes on the bed and floor which made him forget his evening experiences completely.

"Great Scot!" he cried aloud, "did I buy all those things? There'll be a howling big bill to pay when my next month's salary comes, and no mistake."

Then with the pleasure of a child he gave himself up to the investigation of his purchases. Most of the things were Christmas presents he had that afternoon purchased for his friends and the various members of his family. He felt a deep sense of satisfaction in their fineness and beauty as he opened first one and then another. He had done the thing up fine this time as became a young man who was away from home in business for the first time in his life and getting what in the eyes of his family was an exceedingly large salary for one who had been a boy but the other day.

There was the silk dress for mother. He had always said he would buy his mother a silk dress when he got a chance, and he had saved for this for several months. He felt its rich shining folds with clumsy inexperienced fingers and shook it out in a lustrous heap over the bed to admire it. It was all right, for he had asked Frances to tell him just what was the suitable thing for his mother, and she had said black *peau de soie,* and he had carried samples for her inspection one evening when he called, and she had bent over them and studied and talked wisely of texture and wear while the soft light from the opal lamp shone on her pretty hair, and he had thought how sensible she was to advise for the medium price, even though her father was reported to be a millionaire. He smiled at the innocent silk on the bed as though it brought a vision of Frances.

For his sister Mildred he had bought Hoffman's boy head of Christ. He knew that she fancied this particular picture and wanted it. It wasn't exactly the picture he would have selected for her if she had not expressed a strong desire for it, but it was a pretty thing and he placed it on his mantel and surveyed it pleasantly and critically, and as he did so something in the frank, deep gaze of the boy in the picture reminded him of the strange meeting he had attended that evening and the new thoughts that had been stirred by it. Somehow a wave of compunction went through his conscience as he turned back to the new possessions on the bed and remembered the paltry fifty cents he had put in the collection plate.

Last of all of his purchases came the article which had
cost him the most thought and care in selection. It was
a delicate little bronze statue, fine of workmanship and
yet not speaking too loudly of its price to be in keeping
with the position and salary of the donor, and it was
intended for Frances. After all, he acknowledged to
himself, this was the gift in which he took the most
pleasure, this was for the friend—the dearest—and he
drew his breath quickly as he dared to say it to himself,
and wondered what she would think if she knew he
thought in this way about her. Then the eyes of the
picture drew his irresistibly and, as he looked up, by
some queer twist of memory, or hidden law of connec-
tion, there came to his mind the song that had been
sung that evening:

> *I gave my life for thee,*
> *What hast thou given for me?*

and, closely following upon the thought it brought,
came the verses he had learned from the Bible long ago:

> *There is a Friend that sticketh closer than a brother.*

It came with startling clearness, as if it would remind
him that there was a Friend whom he had forgotten, left
out of his Christmas list after all, the very one for whom
the Christmas festival was made in the beginning.

He sat down bewildered, and all the pretty prideful
gifts he had arrayed stared back reproachfully at him. He
sat ashamed before the pictured Christ.

In the sudden sense of shame that had come upon

Gordon he looked away from the things he had bought so proudly but a few hours before, annoyed and unhappy, only to see what he had not noticed before, a chair on the other side of the room also piled high with packages. There was a large suit box, two of them in fact, and a hat box, with several paper parcels. They bore the advertisement of a firm of clothiers and men's furnishing goods on their covers.

The blood flamed high in the young man's face. He felt as if suddenly brought before a court of justice and convicted. These things were all for himself.

That great pile! And fifty cents in the collection basket the only thing he had shown as a Christmas gift to the Saviour of the world—his Saviour, for so in his heart he counted Christ.

He had a generous nature. He liked to give—when he had plenty to give from. He had never considered it so necessary to give very much toward religious institutions until tonight. Why was it that these thoughts were crowding out all the pleasure he was having in his purchases and the anticipated delight in giving them?

He turned impatiently and drew the chair-ful toward him with a jerk. He cut the strings viciously and unwrapped the parcels. Neckties! Why did he want more neckties! His bureau was simply swarming with them now in all the hues of the rainbow. But these were so pretty and so unusual! And just the colors Frances liked—and Frances had said those shades were becoming to him. Well, they were small things to scowl over. He tossed them gloomily aside.

Gloves! Yes, he must have new gloves to wear to the oratorio with Frances the night after Christmas. But he didn't need to buy two pairs just now. He could have waited for the others until after Christmas, and they would have been cheaper then, too.

The raincoat he had perjured his conscience to buy because it was a sample bargain and the last one of the lot, cut in a most unusual way, imported from one of London's great tailors, so the salesman had told him; that raincoat was disappointing now he looked at it with dull, critical eyes. It lay in a limp heap in the box with none of the crisp style to it that had charmed him when he saw it in the store and fancied himself swinging in its embrace down the Avenue holding an umbrella over Frances. He slid the box along on the carpet with the toe of his shoe, and opened the other box. He half hoped that the suit that he had had sent up would not fit. His old one would have done well enough for the oratorio of course, only this one had attracted him, and in the store he had felt quite virtuous to be buying a ready-made suit instead of one made to order, as Frances' brothers always did. Now it seemed even his virtue was an error. He sighed deeply and turned to the hat box for comfort.

To take Frances to the oratorio with this crown of well-dressed manhood upon his head was the fulfillment of a dream he had long dreamed. But now he took the hat from its box with little of the elation he had expected to feel. Somehow he did not like to look at the picture on the mantel and think of the souls without knowledge of Christ that he had heard about that evening, while he held that costly top-piece in his hand. After all, was a high hat so very desirable as he had thought? Was it as necessary to his earthly happiness as it had seemed but that afternoon?

He wished he had never seen it. He put the hat on his head viciously and glared at himself in the mirror, but the reflection did not do justice to his anticipation. He took it off and settled it on again, and looked at it critically, wondering if it was not a little too small, or maybe a little too large, and then threw it back ungently into the box and sat himself down to think.

He was unhappy! He felt that the only thing that could take this unhappiness away was to make it right with his conscience in some way. The only way to do that would be to give a goodly sum as a Christmas gift to that missionary or some other religious cause, he didn't care what. He felt mean, and that was the truth of the matter. He did not stop to tell himself that he had passed many Christmases before without a thought of giving a gift to Christ and been none the worse for it. Over and over until it came to be a din in his ears did that tenor voice ring.

> *I gave my life for thee,*
> *What hast thou given for me?*

He felt that he could not bear that reproach. Well, then, he must reconstruct his list. Perhaps he would have to change some of his presents for cheaper ones and get a little money in that way. He glanced up at the mantel instinctively. The little statue posed in its costly elegance. Not that! He could not change that. Frances headed his list. He could not make her present one whit less costly or beautiful, for she was dearest—here he paused. Was he setting Frances above his Lord? And could he hope to be blest in trying to win her love if he did so? This was not a thought of his own. He distinctly felt it was not. It was sent.

He looked hopelessly at the bright little things strewed about the bed. After all, was that giving a gift to take it out of his other friend's? Had he any right to deprive them of their gifts? Ought it not to be a gift from himself rather than one cut off from what he had intended giving all his friends? And the gift to Christ should have come first in the planning. Christ should always stand first. Had he nothing he could give? Some sacrifice? Was there anything he had that he might sell, or—stay! There were the gold cuff buttons he bought last week. He had never worn them. They were three dollars and a half and were charged on father's bill. He could return them and have them credited, and that would be so much toward a gift to Christ. It would not seem as if the fifty cents stood so very much alone. But still, taken in contrast with the goodly gifts that lay about the room it was small and mean for the Christ of heaven—his Saviour.

Again the heap of clothing he had shoved aside called his attention. Those things were bought and paid for. He told them decidedly they could not be taken back. He was a stranger at that store. How would he look returning all those things? They would think he was crazy. But even as he thought this he remembered that the salesman had told him that he could return the suit if it did not fit and the raincoat had been spoken of in the same way. The salesman had said that if he did not like it on looking it over he could bring it back.

Then began a fight that lasted far into the night. Once or twice as he turned in his restless pacing to and fro he caught a glimpse of the face in the picture he had bought for his sister, and a fierce wish came over him to take that back where it came from. It had been the cause of all his trouble after all. But his better self knew this was folly, and the fight went on between himself and his selfishness.

At first it seemed to him that he was only giving room to an idle thought that troubled him and was trying to explain it all right to himself, but it did not explain. The more he thought about it the more there seemed to be something morally wrong about a professed Christian giving goodly gifts to those who needed them not, and buying fine raiment for himself and giving *nothing* to the Lord. The more this thought became clear to his mind, the more irritated he became, until suddenly facing his mirror, he saw his troubled, angry face full of petulant, childish self-will. Then, and behind it, reflected from the picture on the mantel, was the clear-eyed, boyish face of the pictured Christ, serene in the contemplation of matters of the Kingdom and his Father's business.

Himself in contrast with the Christ was something Gordon Pierce had never thought of before. He was startled. Not so much in the difference of the outward expression of his face and that of the picture, but in the character that both revealed.

He went back to his chair and dropped his face in his hands, and to his startled understanding there came a vision of the man he ought to be beside the man he was. For a little while the first question that had troubled him was lost sight of in the deeper thoughts that stirred his soul to their very depths. Even Frances was forgotten for the time while his soul met God and learned wherein he was found wanting.

A little while later he arose and reverently knelt beside his chair. It was the first thoughtful and unhurried prayer he had uttered since he was a little child and had needed something very much from God.

"Oh, Christ!" he prayed. "I have not been worth much as a Christian. I've been thinking too much about my own pleasure. Forgive me, and help me to do better. I give myself to Thee as a Christmas gift tonight. It is a poor gift, but make it worth something for Thee."

When he got up from his knees he quietly and deliberately picked up the raincoat, the new suit, the neckties and the gloves and carefully folding them laid each in its individual box or paper as it had come. Over the hat he hesitated a moment, started to put it on again, and then abruptly put it in the box and tied the cover down. After that he went to bed.

In the brilliancy of the clear, cold morning that succeeded the night of storm, he started down-town an hour earlier than usual, his arms laden with many bundles. His fellow boarders eyed him curiously, for he did not usually burden himself with anything when he started out in the morning. He affected an elegant leisure in all his ways. This was not because of his upbringing, but because he had supposed it would beget him a dignity in keeping with one who aspired to friendship with one like Frances. But this morning he had forgotten all such thoughts; his set face showed determination and a will that would carry it out.

From counter to counter, from one department to another in the great store he went. He blessed the happy custom that made it possible for him to return these ill-advised purchases without wranglings and explanations.

When he reached the last place, however, and opened the box containing the beloved hat, the young salesman who had waited upon him happened to be sauntering near the exchange desk and recognized him. He raised his eyebrows slightly as he glanced significantly at the hat, and said enquiringly: "What's the matter? Didn't it fit?"

The blood flushed the customer's cheek and he felt as guilty as though he had stolen the hat. He answered unconcernedly: "I've decided to do without it." But he felt as though the whole miserable business was written on his face.

He was glad when his hands were empty and the money he had received in exchange for the various packages he had brought down-town was safely in his pocket. He counted it up mentally as he boarded the car that went toward his office, inwardly thankful that there was not much doing in his business this cold weather, and his presence at the office at an early hour was not so necessary as it would have been at another season of the year.

When he reached the office he found the general manager had been there and ordered some of the men off to another part of the city, and there would be nothing for him to do that morning. He sat at his desk for a little while doing some figuring and counting his money. At last with a happy face he counted out thirty dollars and rolled it together by itself. Then he took up the morning paper and turned to the notices of religious services held the night before. It took him some time to find the mention of the meeting he had attended, but at last he found it in an obscure corner. It gave him what he wanted, however, the name of the man who had spoken so eloquently about missions and the name of the pastor in whose church the meeting was held.

With a brighter face he donned his overcoat and hat once more and hailing an up-town car was soon on his way to find the pastor. He was not at home, but his wife came to see the caller and explained that he would be away for a couple of days.

This was disappointment. When Gordon Pierce did anything he wanted to do it at once. Somehow those heathen in India would weigh on his soul and remind him of his lost high hat until the money he had decided to send them was out of his keeping. He drew his brows in perplexity. It had seemed too easy to hunt up this minister and ask him to send the money to the man who had spoken the evening before. The minister's wife studied the handsome young face before her and her heart went out in sympathy. She was used to helping young people through all sorts of trying times, from getting married to getting out of jail, so she asked a simple question sympathetically, and he opened his heart to her at once, glad of a way out. Her face brightened as she heard that it was money for the missionary.

"Oh, then, it will be all right!" she said eagerly. "Just take it to Mr. Adamson. He is the treasurer of our church and has charge of the money for Dr. Hanson's work. You will find him at his office on Chestnut Street. You know Adamson and Co. Just ask for Mr. Adamson, senior. I am so glad there is someone interested enough to take the trouble to bring some money. It was an interesting meeting last night, was it not? Too bad there were not more out, but, then, it was wretched weather and so near to Christmas, too. People are selfish at Christmas in spite of everything. They will not come out or give. It was not a good time for a missionary meeting anyway, but we could not get Dr. Hanson any other time. Good morning. I am glad you have called. I will tell my husband."

She bowed and smiled him out. He went down and gave his thirty dollars to the surprised Mr. Adamson, who looked with his keen business eyes at the young man glowing in the fervor of his first sacrifice for Christ, and wondered, but took the money and made a record of it with the name of the giver.

It was the night of the oratorio, and Gordon Pierce, with many a sigh, for the glow of sacrifice does not always last through the real part of the sacrifice itself, had arrayed himself in his old clothes, which were not so old except in comparison with new ones, and had donned his hat with many a thought of the hat that might have been, and gone after Miss Frances. He had been invited to sit in their own private box with the family, and he knew it was a great honor. He always felt that when the sharp gaze of Frances' father rested upon him every defect of his life stood out in bold relief, and so he had been particularly anxious to appear as well as possible, for with Frances' father rested, after all, the final giving away of Frances herself to any young man, no matter how much he might love her or she love him.

And very nice indeed he looked as he sat beside her waving her unnecessary little fan just for sheer pleasure of doing something for her. Frances' father sat watching him critically and could not deny that he was handsome, but wished that he would not look so ardently into that beloved daughter's face. He had happened to pass through a store and had seen the young gentleman trying on a high hat, and Frances' father was a self-made man. He knew what high silk hats cost, and he happened to know the size of Gordon Pierce's salary. He could not forget that hat. He expected to have it in evidence very conspicuously this evening, but had been surprised to find that the young man did not wear it, and took pains to keep his hat out of sight. His observations at this point were interrupted by Mr. Adamson, his friend, who had seen him in the audience and at the intermission came over to the box to consult him about something important. The business finished, Mr. Adamson glanced up at the young man beside Frances.

"By the way," said he, "who is that young man?"

"That?" said the father, dejectedly brought back to the thorn that had been troubling him. "That is a young kid who thinks the universe centers around Frances. His name is Pierce. He is a civil engineer and doing well, but I'm afraid there isn't much in him."

"Well, he did not strike me as that kind," said Mr. Adamson decidedly.

"Where did you meet him? What do you know of him?" asked Frances' father.

"He came to see me two or three days ago to give me

some money for Dr. Hanson's mission. What did you say his salary was? I asked him if he was giving it himself, and he said, 'Yes.' "

"You don't say!" murmured Frances' father, turning and regarding the flushed young man with a new interest. It was characteristic of Frances' father that he requested young Mr. Pierce to call at his office the next day.

"Young man,"—the millionaire knew how to come directly to a point when he saw one—"where did you get that thirty dollars to give to missions?" he asked abruptly.

It seemed to Gordon that every folly and every tender feeling of his heart was to be stripped from him here and now, and he stood trembling as one condemned. He felt a sudden desire to cry as when a small boy he had seen the big boys run off with all the fun after he had helped work to get it. Then a rare quality of his came to the front, and he saw the funny side of the whole thing.

"From the fine clothes that I didn't buy," he answered with a choking laugh. "There was a high hat and an imported raincoat and a new suit and a lot of neckties."

"H'm!" said the old man, regarding him severely, "and what did you want all those things for?"

"To appear well before your daughter, sir."

"Indeed! And why didn't you get them?" The face grew quizzical.

A glow came into Gordon's eyes. "I did buy them," he answered quietly.

"What! Then how did you get the money back?"

"I bought them and had them sent home. Then I

went to that meeting; the storm sent me in. It was not my own doing. I thought perhaps God sent me."

There was something grim in the older man's face. He had heard sentimentalists talk of God's doings in their lives before, and blame their own weaknesses on a higher power.

"I heard that man talk about those people who do not know about the Gospel. I heard some singing, too. I know you will not understand how I was stirred by it. Perhaps it will seem weak to you, but when I got home I got to thinking about it all, and looking over the things I had bought for myself and what I got for Christmas for my friends, Father and Mother and my sister—and the best I could afford for your daughter, for Frances, and something reminded me that I had given nothing to Christ. I can't explain to you, sir. It was only just that I felt that I had not been doing right by the Lord. I've never been any great Christian, but I never felt so cheap in my life as I did that night. So the next morning I took all the things back that I had bought for myself and I figured up and found just how much money I could spare and yet get through the month; and I hunted up the man who talked and gave him the money. I don't see how you found out about it, sir." There was quiet respect in Gordon Pierce's tones as he finished.

The old man wore a curious look of grim satisfaction. "H'm!" he said at last, after calmly surveying his visitor. "And might I presume to enquire why you wished to appear well before my daughter?"

"Because I love her."

The face of Frances' father softened about the grim

mouth and keen eyes. He was remembering his own youth.

"And had you ceased to love her when you took back your fine clothes?"

"No," said he, "I loved her all the more, but I loved Christ best. I had bought your daughter's Christmas gift, but I had nothing for my Lord."

"Well," said the old man, turning toward his desk, "you did well. Perhaps you won't mind adding a little from me to that Christmas present you gave." He was writing in his checkbook now as if nothing had happened. The young man looked at him curiously and wondered how he should say what he must say before he left that office.

"There, I'll trouble you to hand that to Mr. Adamson from me to go with yours to missions. I don't mind encouraging a Christmas gift like that. I'll go without a high hat myself another year," and he chuckled dryly, and rubbed his hands together.

Gordon Pierce studied the check in his hands bewilderingly. It was filled out for three hundred dollars made payable to Mr. Adamson. His face brightened as he suddenly understood. He was glad beyond measure to have his gift recognized by one so much larger, and he felt the joy of the old man's approval. But there was something else he must ask before this interview ended.

He went over by the millionaire's desk and dared to grasp the hand that had held so many dollars. "Sir, I have told you that I love your daughter. I want to tell you that I am going to try to make her love me. Have I your permission to do so?"

The hands were clasped for a moment while the old eyes looked long into the young ones.

"Well, I guess you can do it, my boy. Go ahead."

Alone in his own room that night Gordon's first act was to kneel and thank his heavenly Father for the great gift of a woman's love that had been bestowed upon him. Then in glad resolve to make this new year a new life in every way he took down his neglected Bible and turning over the leaves, scarcely knowing how to begin a long broken habit, he lighted upon these words:

"Give and it shall be given to you—good measure, pressed down, shaken together and running over, shall men give into your bosom. For with the same measure you mete withal it shall be measured to you again."

Reverently he bowed his head as he realized that even then all gifts of his would never requite the great gift God had given to him that night.

Grace Livingston Hill
1865–1947

Grace Livingston Hill was born in Wellsville, New York, and lived most of her life in Swarthmore, Pennsylvania. A prolific columnist, short-story writer, and novelist, she is significant for another reason: Her books have not only stayed in print but have also gained in popularity during the half century since her death. Her books include *Cloudy Jewel* (1920), *The Beloved Stranger* (1933), *Rainbow Cottage* (1934), *White Orchids* (1935), *April Gold* (1936), *The Substitute Guest* (1936), and *Brentwood* (1937).

Joseph A. MacDougall
(AS TOLD TO DOUGLAS HOW)

HOW AN UNBORN BABY SAVED ITS MOTHER'S LIFE

This Christmas story, told by a respected physician who practiced in the Maritime Provinces in the last half of the twentieth century, is unlike any other I have ever seen. In fact, it more than borders—it crosses over—the impossible. Yet, the fact is that it happened.

$\mathcal{F}$inally, one day that December, I had to tell her. Medically, we were beaten. The decision lay with God. She took it quietly, lying there, wasting away, only 23, and the mother of a year-old child. Eleanor Munro (the name has been changed) was a devout and courageous woman. She had red hair and had probably been rather pretty, but it was hard to tell anymore, she was that near to death from tuberculosis. She knew it now, she accepted it, and just asked for one thing.

"If I'm still alive on Christmas Eve," she said slowly, "I would like your promise that I can go home for Christmas."

It disturbed me. I knew she shouldn't go. The lower lobe of her right lung had a growing tubercular cavity in it, roughly one inch in diameter. She had what the doctors call open TB, and could spread the germs by coughing. But I made the promise and, frankly, I did so because I was sure she'd be dead before Christmas Eve. In the circumstances, it seemed little enough to do. And if I hadn't made it, I wouldn't be telling this story now.

Eleanor's husband had the disease when he returned to Nova Scotia from overseas service in World War II. It was a mild case and he didn't know he had it. Before it was detected and checked, they married. She caught the disease and had little immunity against it. It came on so fast and lodged in such a difficult place that it confounded every doctor who tried to help her.

To have a tubercular cavity in the lower lobe is rare. When they took her to the provincial sanitarium in Kentville, it quickly became obvious that the main problem was how to get at it. If it had been in the upper lobe, they could have performed an operation called thoracoplasty, which involves taking out some of the upper ribs to collapse the lobe, and put that area of the lung at rest. Unfortunately, this operation couldn't be used for the lower lobe because it would have meant removing some of the lower ribs, which her body needed for support, and in any case probably would not collapse the cavity.

With thoracoplasty ruled out, they tried a process called artificial pneumothorax, which employs needles to pump in air to force collapse of the lung through pressure. Although several attempts were made, this process didn't work because previous bouts of pleurisy had stuck the lung to the chest wall, and the air couldn't circulate.

Finally they considered a then-rare surgical procedure called pneumonectomy—taking out the entire lung— but rejected it because she was too sick to withstand surgery, and steadily getting worse. Their alternatives exhausted, they reluctantly listed her as a hopeless case and sent her back to her home hospital in Antigonish.

I was 31 then and I hadn't been there very long when she arrived. I graduated from Dalhousie University's medical school in 1942, joined the Royal Canadian Air Force, and then completed my training as an anaesthetist in Montreal once the war was over. A native of Sydney, N.S., I accepted a position with St. Martha's Hospital in Antigonish. I was to provide an anaesthesia service and take care of the medical needs of the students at two local colleges. I was also asked to look after a small TB annex at the hospital, a place for about 40 patients, most of them chronics with little or no hope of being cured.

That's how Eleanor Munro came to be my patient in 1947.

She had weighed 125 pounds. She was down to 87 the first time I saw her. Her fever was high, fluctuating between 101 and 103 degrees. She was, and looked, very toxic. But she could still smile. That, I'll always remember. If you did her the slightest kindness, she'd smile.

Maybe that encouraged me. I don't know. But I did know then that I had to try to help her.

I first called Dr. I. Rabinovitch in Montreal because he was a top expert on the use of the then-new drug streptomycin. Early information was that, in certain circumstances, it might help cure TB. Dr. Rabinovitch told me the drug wasn't available. When I described the case he said he would advise against its use anyway. I then phoned a doctor in New York who was experimenting with a procedure called pneumoperitoneum.

Pneumoperitoneum consists of injecting needles into the peritoneal cavity to force in air and push the diaphragm up against the lung. If we could get pressure against that lower lobe, we could hope to force the TB cavity shut. If we could do that, nature would have a chance to close and heal the cavity by letting the sides grow together.

At the hospital, we considered the risks and decided we had to face them. The operation took place the day after my phone call. We pumped air into the peritoneal cavity, but it nearly killed her. It was obvious that the amount of air she could tolerate could in no way help.

Every doctor in the room agreed we shouldn't try a second time. We were licked.

It was then that I told her medical science had gone as far as it could go. I explained why in detail and she appreciated it. She listened with a quiet dignity and an amazing resignation. I told her that her Creator now had the final verdict and that it would not necessarily be what either of us wanted, but would be the best for her under the circumstances. She nodded, and then exacted from me that promise.

Amazingly, she was still alive on Christmas Eve, but just barely. The cavity was still growing; her condition still worsening. But she held me to my promise and, with renewed doubts, I kept it. I told her not to hold her child and to wear a surgical mask if she was talking to anyone but her husband. His own case had given him immunity.

She promised and off she went by ambulance, wearing that smile I can't forget.

She came back to St. Martha's late Christmas Day, and she kept ebbing. No one could have watched her struggle without being deeply moved. Every day her condition grew just a bit worse, yet every day she clung to life. It went on, to our continued amazement, for weeks.

Toward the end of February she was down to or below 80 pounds; she couldn't eat—and new complications developed. She became nauseous, began to retch and vomit even without food in her stomach. I was stumped. I called in a senior medical consultant and when he examined her he was stumped too. But with a grin, almost facetiously, he asked me if I thought she could be pregnant.

I can still remember exactly how I felt: the suggestion was utterly ridiculous. Everything I knew about medicine added up to one conclusion: she was so ill, so weak that she couldn't possibly have conceived. Her body just wasn't up to it. Nevertheless I did take a pregnancy test—and to my astonishment it was positive. On the very outer frontier of life itself she now bore a second life within her. It was about as close to the impossible as you're ever likely to get, but it was true.

When I told her she smiled and sort of blushed.

Legally, medically, we could have taken that child through abortion because it imperilled a life that was already in jeopardy. At that time TB was the No. 1 medical reason for doing so. But we didn't do it. The patient and her husband were against it. We doctors at St. Martha's were against it, not only on religious grounds, but because we were certain the operation would kill her. Besides, she was so far gone, we were sure her body would reject the child anyway.

So we fed her intravenously, and watched her fight to sustain two lives in a body in which only some remarkable strength of character or divine intervention had allowed her to sustain even one.

The struggle went on for weeks, and never once did we alter our conviction that she was dying. And she kept her child. And then an incredible thing began to happen. By late March, 1948, I was confounded to find her temperature beginning to go down. For the first time we noted some improvement in her condition, and the improvement continued. She began to eat, and to gain weight. A chest x-ray showed that the growth of the TB cavity had stopped. Not long after, another x-ray showed that the diaphragm was pushing up against the lower lobe of her diseased lung to make room for the child she bore. Nature was doing exactly what we'd failed to do with pneumoperitoneum: it was pressing the sides of that deadly hole together. The child was saving the mother!

The child did save her. By the time it was born, a normal healthy baby, the TB cavity was closed. The mother was markedly better, so much better that we let her go home for good within a few months. Her smile had never been brighter.

I still find it hard to believe, and I've never heard of a comparable case since. I never discussed it with the young woman, even when she came in for checkups which confirmed the full return of good health. And never, until recently, have I cited the case publicly to make a point. The child didn't destroy its mother. It saved her. Call it the will of God, call it human love, call it the mystic quality of motherhood, the turning in upon herself to fight still more because she had still more to fight for, call it what you will: it happened. It doesn't matter if it never happens again. Indeed, it is not likely to happen again now that we have the drugs to cure tubercular cases like hers, but that's not the point. It happened, and it happened, I'm convinced, because there is a force in nature, a wisdom, a balance, a mystery beyond man's comprehension—and man should recognize and accept it.

If I need any convincing, that woman convinced me. I still wonder at what she did and at the unfathomable force it signifies. And I still remember with delight the Christmas cards she sent me for years. They were just ordinary cards, with the usual printed greetings and her name. But, to me, they were like monuments to a miracle of Christmas.

Dr. Joseph A. MacDougall

The late Dr. Joseph A. MacDougall was one of the most distinguished anesthesiologists to have practiced in the Maritime Provinces during the last half century.

Douglas How

Douglas How's long and illustrious career has spanned more than half a century writing for many Canadian magazines and newspapers, including the Canadian *Reader's Digest*. He still lives and writes from his native New Brunswick.

A CHRISTMAS EXPERIENCE

Miss Martin's heart-touchingly lovely voice moved the great congregation deeply. Effusively was she praised.

Ah, but to also sing at the penitentiary? Unthinkable!

*A*s Miss Martin passed into the side entrance that led to the choir loft, she overheard a murmur from the group of people on the pavement, "That is she—our first soprano that I told you about. I can hardly wait for you to hear her glorious voice."

A slight flush mounted her face, and a feeling that she deserved the words of praise swelled in her heart. Had she not struggled up through many a trial to her pleasant high place in the musical world? Now that success was hers she should enjoy it to the full. She loosened the rich fur that clasped her throat and removed the filmy veil that protected her wavy hair from the rough caresses of the wind, unrolled her music, and softly trilled a bar or two— not because she needed further preparation, but from the very joy of being able to warble like a bird. If the people of this church had liked her voice before, what would they think after the magnificent solo she would sing that Christmas morning?

Just then Mr. Niles came into the ante-room behind the great organ. "Miss—Martin?"

"Well?" she said, smiling encouragingly.

"I want to ask a favor of you. A few of us are going this afternoon to the women's ward of the penitentiary to hold a service with the inmates. Could you—would you go with us and sing for them?"

"Why, Mr. Niles, how dreadful!"

"What is dreadful?"

"The whole idea, the penitentiary—ugh. And this day of all days to visit such a ghastly place. You must excuse me."

"Miss Martin, if you understood all it would mean to those poor creatures—some of them young, most of them victims of circumstance, rather than criminals from choice, I think you would go. It is just an hour—then there are twenty-three hours of Christmas left, you know."

The organ was pealing, and its deep tones reverberated among the huge pipes. Miss Martin laid her hand on the door knob. "I shall need the afternoon for rest and preparation for the song service tonight. Someone else can sing for you—they have less to do than I have," and Mr. Niles was left alone, while Miss Martin took her place in the choir loft. The service moved on smoothly—the hymn, prayer, the anthems and the scripture lesson; and then her solo—the event of the morning to others than the singer. It was all she had hoped and more. The audience sat through it spellbound, and many were in tears as the last note died slowly away.

Miss Martin did not expect to pay much heed to the sermon—the important part of the morning had ended when her work was done. But she had not counted on the effect of Mr. Niles' earnest prayer for her out in the little ante-room after she left him, nor on the message which the minister, filled with the Spirit, brought from God to her soul.

It was over at last and she went out, only pausing to say, "Mr. Niles, I have changed my mind. You may count on me this afternoon." He looked after her in pleased surprise, but she pulled down her veil and was gone.

So it came about that she was one of the little group who filed into the penitentiary hall that afternoon and stood facing the row upon row of women sitting there in prison garb.

On all four sides wound stairways leading to the grated cells four tiers high. At the front of the hall stood a white pulpit, a small organ and several chairs. Doors were locked, windows barred, inside were wretchedness and misery; outside the blessed freedom of God's pure air and Christmas. Sitting during the opening exercise, Miss Martin scanned the faces of those in front of her; some so pitifully young and fair, and some as free from marks of guilt as hers; others hard and old in sin, with evil eyes and darkened brows.

On the front row sat a woman not more than thirty-five years old, but with a seamed and hardened face looking sadly out of keeping with her crimped and frizzed hair which towered above her forehead. She stared with sullen, glittering eyes at Mr. Niles as he read and prayed. Many heads were bowed and sounds of stifled sobbing came from different parts of the room as the sweet story of the risen Lord was read, but this woman sat like a statue with compressed lips.

Then Miss Martin sang. Those walls had never echoed to sounds more sweet, for her heart was in the message as she sang of Jesus—His love and pity. The black eyes did not leave her face, nor give any sign of feeling. While Mr. Niles and others talked, Miss Martin's heart was lifted in prayer, the first real prayer she had ever uttered, it seemed to her—that God would give her the joy of bearing a message of help to some needy soul.

At the request that those who wished to be prayed for should make it known, many hands were raised and yearning faces were uplifted, as if pleading for help. But the woman on the front seat did not move, nor take her steady gaze from the beautiful girlish face by the organ.

She sang again—a message of peace on earth, good will to men, so sadly needed. As she finished, the black eyes dimmed suddenly and the set lips whispered, "Oh, sing again, sing again!"

She began at once the gospel hymn: "Softly and Tenderly Jesus Is Calling." Every sentence thrilled with entreaty, as she sang, "Come home, come home." As she finished, the hardened face suddenly melted and a broken voice sobbed out, "Help me, oh, help me! I do want to be good." On the stone floor they knelt and there with deep penitence and earnest entreaty at last one sinful soul found forgiveness.

"It was the singing that did it," the poor woman said, holding fast to the firm white hand that did not shrink from the contact. "I could have resisted all the rest, but not that—on this day of all days, Christ's birthday—and mine."

The voice sank to a whisper, but the once hard face now glowed with the light of Christmas.

Margaret E. Sangster, Jr.

LIKE A CANDLE IN
THE WINDOW

Joan Carter was sick and tired of being married to a man who seemingly belonged more to his church parishioners than he did to her. She determined that next year she'd go home. Not to this home—back east to her parents. But then there was a knock on the door.

*G*reg lifted her tenderly across the threshold of the little gray stone house, and held her tightly in his arms. Her clear blue eyes looked up into his, and then suddenly she buried her head in the fold of his arm and sobbed out—

"Oh, Gregory Carter, I love you—love you with all my heart, but I wish I didn't."

"Well, Mrs. Carter, for a bride of two weeks—that is quite a statement. Would you mind telling me why you wish you didn't love your husband?"

"All my life I've told myself, *Joan, don't ever marry a preacher—marry a lawyer, a farmer, a tailor, a baker, but don't ever marry a preacher.* And here I am—married to you, the pastor of a church in a little mountain town a thousand miles from nowhere—and I want a husband— a husband all my own!"

"Any complaints so far?" smiled Gregory. "You have had my entire and undivided attention for the past two weeks. I thought we had quite a honeymoon."

Joan snuggled her head into the spot between Greg's ear and his collarbone.

"I've loved every minute of the past two weeks, but that is just it. For two weeks I have had a wonderful husband who gave me his undivided love and attention, but for the rest of my life I must share you with every-body—your whole congregation and anyone else who needs you. I'm tired of your people! They met us at the station and drove us from one end of the town to the other. My hand aches from being squeezed, I'm gummy from being kissed by women I've never seen before. Probably they're looking at us right now—staring through the windows, three or four of them in my kitchen—watching! I feel as if we would live in a glass house for the rest of our lives!"

There was a creak somewhere in the back of the house and involuntarily Greg glanced back over his shoulder. Joan's sobs stopped abruptly, she dabbed at her eyes with a handkerchief and called, "Come on out— come out wherever you are."

The hall door opened and they streamed in, laughing and calling, "Welcome home!"

The senior deacon, the junior deacon, and their wives and children, the Dorcas and the choir. They were all there, and they had food—pies, cakes and sandwiches. Greg went forward to greet them and they gathered around him.

They love Greg, thought Joan. *He's their pastor. Oh, make me strong enough to accept them!* And then suddenly she was angry. *Greg's my husband! He belongs to me. It's our life and we are going to live it.*

They left finally, and Joan sank down on the living room sofa. The room was a mess. Dirty cups and plates sticky with cake frosting—half eaten sandwiches curling up at the edges.

Greg said gently, "The women will come back tomorrow—they'll clean everything up."

"But, I don't want them to come back! I want to wash my own dishes and clean my own house."

Greg laughed. "You were an only child, darling— you've never learned to share."

"But, Greg, you'll never belong entirely to me. I want a husband who goes to work at eight and comes home at five, and between five and eight will belong to me."

"I'll always belong to you, dear. We both belong to our Heavenly Father and because we do, we belong to each other. You will find that love is like the widow's meal: the more you give, the more you have for yourself. Life in this secluded little community is hard and dull, and oh, my dear, we have so much to give. Our lives must be like a guiding star—like a candle in a window—to show those who pass by the way home."

And so they settled down—the young Carters—Gregory Carter and his wife Joan—living indeed in a gold fish bowl in a small mountain village. Living in a stone house, separated from a stone church by twenty paces of snowy lawn.

Greg preached fervently and honestly from the pulpit. He drove out into the country to call on the sick parishioners, to perform marriage services and pray above open graves. And Joan, at home, did her best to keep the parsonage shining, to cook meals that were nourishing and edible, to think according to the pattern of her new life. She had a ceaseless stream of callers—somebody every day. Mrs. Judson, across the street—"You say you were born in New York City? My, my, how you must miss the bright lights and all the goin's on. Nothin' but God's mountains to look at here, and Main Street." And Joan would murmur, "It's a charming little town."

"That coat you wore to church last Sunday, Honey, was it real mink or muskrat?"

"Mink," Joan would nod. "Daddy gave it to me when I was eighteen."

Or Mrs. Tenney from around the corner would drop in to help her dry the dishes and exclaim, "Land sakes, Dearie! You don't use these fancy dishes every day, I hope!"

And Joan would answer, "Yes, they were wedding gifts, and I like to use them."

When Joan protested to her husband that she was tired of all the women giving her advice and prying into her own personal affairs, Greg answered, "Darling, the city you came from is made up of many little islands, and on each island people live by and to themselves. But it's different when you live in a small town. It's all one island, and you're common property."

When they had been married for one month, Joan thought it called for a celebration and baked a pie, her very first. It was lemon meringue, and it was beautiful. That evening she set the table with their best china and silver. She gathered flowers and placed them in the center of the table with a tall candle at either end. The table was beautiful and the dinner was delicious. Joan was thinking, *How wonderful to have an evening all to ourselves.*

She had just cleared the plates away and was going for her triumph, the lemon meringue pie, to set before her husband, when there was a knock at the door. Answering, Greg heard, "Gooda evening—you are ze meenister, please? I am Tony and this is Maria—we like to get married please."

"Get married?" asked Greg. "Are you alone? Where are your families?"

"Oh, please, we have no families. You see, I come

five year ago from Italy. All ze time I maka ze shoes, every day I maka shoes, maka shoes, and sava my money. Till at last I have enough to bring Maria. She is all ze time waiting in ze old country. And now, today, she comes. I gotta ze house ready. Oh, we are very happy, and now we lika get married please. We have no family in this country—no mamma, no papa, no brother, no sister, just Maria and Tony, thasa all. And now, we lika get married. Too bad no family, but with flowers on the table and candles, justa like nice wedding."

Greg hesitated. "But if Maria has just come, she does not speak English. She will not understand the cere-mony."

"Oh, no matter," answered Tony. "You tella me, I tella Maria. We do okay."

And so with Joan as witness, the service proceeded with Tony translating each vow carefully. And when at last Greg had pronounced them man and wife, Tony smiled at Joan and said hopefully, "Maybe you be like a sister to Maria. She has only me, Tony. No mamma, no sister, in this country." And suddenly Joan remembered the lemon meringue pie. Four of the very best plates were placed on the table and the china cups were filled with steaming chocolate, and the pie that was baked just for two became a wedding feast for four.

Joan did try to be like a sister to Maria. Maria was a beautiful girl, gracious and charming, and Joan enjoyed taking her to the village market and helping her a bit to master the new language. She made it a point to see that she met the other young women in the congregation, and several times Tony and Maria were dinner guests at the parsonage.

But Joan still found it very hard to accept "Greg's people." "Why can't we ever have a little time to ourselves? Why must the house always be filled with your people?" she demanded of Greg.

"They aren't my people, Darling," he answered. "They are God's people, the sheep of His pasture, and it was God who sent us here to be the shepherd of His flock."

And Joan had choked back the tears as she answered, "Maybe He sent you. Oh, if we only had a home—a real home that was all ours. Why must we share everything with your people?"

"Because, Dear, I'm their pastor, and you're their pastor's wife. Whatever is ours must be theirs, too."

The day Greg had promised to take Joan shopping in the city—sixty miles away—just as they were ready to leave, Nash Simpson had come in and said his oldest boy was determined to leave home—that with the summer planting and all, they needed him desperately, and besides, what would a boy his age do in the big city—wouldn't Greg come over and talk to him? And Greg had gone and talked until it was too late to make the shopping trip. But he had persuaded the boy to stay and help his father until the harvest was over, and had promised that he would go with him in the fall and help him find work and a place to live in the city, if he still wanted to go.

The night Joan's sister and her husband had stopped to visit them on their way home from a business trip—they were just sitting down to dinner when the doctor

called—Silas Wathers was badly hurt, nearly cut his leg
off with a scythe. Wouldn't the pastor drive out with
the doctor? And Greg had gone, and the sister had
wondered how Joan managed, never being able to
depend on having her husband at home. Joan had lifted
her chin a bit and said, "Oh, that is part of being a
pastor's wife," but she had wondered herself how she
stood it.

When Mr. Carlton, the only wealthy member of the
congregation, gave the church a new organ, Joan was
the only one who could play it; so it was Joan who
played for the choir—and this brought responsibilities
and more people making demands of her, though she
loved the music and devoted much time to planning the
numbers for each service.

Sarah Bradley had finished high school and was to go
in to the State College for the fall term. She appeared at
Joan's door one morning with the catalogue under her
arm. "Oh, Mrs. Carter, won't you help me choose my
clothes? I want to look as nice as the other girls at
school. If you would just help me—you always look so
nice." And Joan had spent the morning with her until
the order was made out—a dress for parties, a neat suit
for church, skirts and blouses and sweaters for school.
And Joan had contributed some gay little scarfs and a
dainty handkerchief. Sarah went home with a light heart
though Joan's ironing was still undone.

"Mrs. Carlton was here today," Joan announced at
dinner a week before Thanksgiving. "She says we must
have Thanksgiving with them, we must go there
directly after the service." She paused, and then, "But
we're not going, Greg. I want to have this Thanksgiving

alone, with you. It will be our first Thanksgiving together, our last as bride and groom, and I want to cook our dinner. I want to serve it on my own dishes to my husband."

"Mr. Carlton is our greatest benefactor," said Greg. "He's also our best friend. It was he, you know, who had the oil burner put in this parsonage. He gave the money for the organ. We'll *have* to go to his house for Thanksgiving, Darling. They have extended the invitation to show their friendship and love for us."

"All right, Greg Carter, you may go and eat Thanksgiving dinner with the Carltons, but *I* am staying home. I married you, not your congregation. It's you I love, not all your people." And so Greg told his senior deacon that Joan was not feeling well, that they would have to decline their invitation. But somehow the dinner was not the success Joan had anticipated.

And then suddenly it was the morning of Christmas Eve, and the sky was a leaden gray. By noon it was snowing, and by late afternoon a blizzard was howling. And Mr. Carlton's gift, the oil burner, wasn't working the way it should. But in spite of the cold, Joan had decorated the room with the evergreen and holly berries Greg had brought in, and a gay little Christmas tree stood in the corner near the window. "Oh, Greg," Joan said, "Christmas is a wonderful time!" And then the telephone rang.

"Darling," said Greg as he returned from the telephone, "you remember old Mr. Murray? He's taken a turn for the worse; he may not live the night out. I must go to him."

"Through this blizzard?" Joan asked. Greg nodded.

"And leave me alone on Christmas Eve?"

"You'll be all right, Darling. Remember we have a lifetime ahead of us to spend Christmas together, and this is perhaps the last one on this earth for Mr. Murray. I must do what I can for him, Dear."

"All right! But this is the last Christmas I'm spending here. I'm going home to my family in New York. How can anybody be happy, married to an impersonal minister who belongs to everybody but his wife?"

So Greg kissed her, held her tightly for a moment, and then started out in his small elderly car; and as the white pencils of snow broke against his windshield, he prayed—for a safe journey, that he might bring strength and courage and faith to Mr. Murray; for Joan's protection and for their happiness. And Joan pressed her nose to the window pane and tried to see across a white world.

"Oh, Greg, Greg, you are so fine and good, but I want you all to myself."

And as she looked, she saw a light coming toward her through the storm. She watched until a knock sounded at the door. "Come in," she called and turned to see Mrs. Tenney. She had come with a loaf of freshly baked bread, warm and fragrant.

"Oh, Mrs. Tenney, you came through the storm to bring this to us!"

"My dear, I had to come. It's Christmas Eve, and I had to come and tell you how much you have done for me during the year. I hope you haven't minded me coming in so often, just in time to dry your dishes. Somehow as I have touched those sparkling glasses and dainty cups it has made me want to keep my hands and heart clean and shining like them. It's made me realize that life isn't all just work and hardship. There is beauty all around us if we just look for it. You can't know what it has meant to come to the parsonage here, so spotless and pretty. This isn't much but I hope you'll enjoy it and know how much we love you."

As Joan stood holding the warm loaf of bread, tears filled her eyes, but she wiped them quickly as a voice called out, "Anybody home?" It was Mrs. Judson from across the street.

"All alone? I thought as much. I knew about old Mr. Murray, and I figured the pastor'd be out there with him. 'Tain't exactly nice to spend Christmas Eve alone, so I just thought I'd run over for a few minutes. My! Your house looks right Christmasy. But then, this house always looks just the way a pastor's home should look. Neat as a pin, flowers here and there for a bit of cheer, and comfortable chairs just where they're needed most. I hope I haven't been a bother to you, but it always just starts my day out right to run over for just a minute or two. And I've said more'n once, it's no wonder our pastor is such a success, always full of courage and cheer. With such a home to come to when his work is over. And your clothes seemed a mite extravagant at first, but more men'd come home if their wives kept themselves prettied up and looked like something worth comin' home to! Oh yes, I've said many a time, says I, 'Our pastor's wife does her part and does it well.' My! I might near forgot, here's a pint of my strawberry preserves. I hope you'll like them."

Sarah Bradley stopped by to show Joan how well her suit fit and to tell her how well she was getting on at college. "Oh, Mrs. Carter, I don't know what I'd ever have done without your help. The girls all like my clothes, and they like me! Oh, I just love you, Mrs. Carter, and I hope I can be just like you someday. I think it would be just wonderful being a minister's wife, everybody loves you so."

Tony and Maria came through the snow to bring a beautiful scarf of dainty handwork. "To say thank you for your kindness," said Maria in her broken English. "You've been like my sister," and she stooped to kiss Joan's hand. And Tony added, "In the spring comes a little bambino, and if it is a girl, we call her Joan. You think the name is good?"

It was Mr. Carlton who stopped next. He came in stamping the snow from his boots. "Well, just stopped in to wish you a Merry Christmas. We won't ask you to spend Christmas with us. Figured maybe you'd like to be alone bein's this is your first Christmas together in your own home. I just had the oil tank filled and left a bushel of apples on the back step. I don't know what we'd do without you and the pastor, Mrs. Carter. You've done a lot for this community. Why, it seems like you've been like a guiding star, like a candle set in a window, to show us poor folks the way. I reckon the pastor is out with old Mr. Murray, figured he'd be there. Well, give him my greetings and don't forget to count on us for anything we can do."

It was almost midnight when Joan heard the car turn in

the driveway. She rushed to the door and opened it to light the way for Greg.

"Well, Darling, I'm home in time for Christmas. Has it been dreadfully lonely? Has it been a terribly long evening for you?"

"I've missed you, Dear; but our people have seen to it that it was not long nor lonely. The house has been filled with them, and who could be lonely when you are surrounded by love and kindness? When you belong to the whole community?"

Greg gathered her into his arms and carried her into the house.

"Oh, Greg, wouldn't it have been terrible if I had married some stuffed shirt of a polo player, or some rising young executive? I love you, Greg Carter, love you with all my heart, and I'm glad, glad, glad that I do. I wouldn't change places with anyone in this whole wide world. I'm going to write to my cousin Rosalie and thank her again for bringing us together."

"It was God who brought us together, Dear. He had His eye on you all the time because He knew you'd make the perfect wife for the pastor of a little church, in a little town, a thousand miles from nowhere."

Margaret E. Sangster, Jr.
1894–1981

Margaret E. Sangster, Jr., granddaughter of the equally illustrious Margaret E. Sangster (1838–1912), was born in Brooklyn, New York. Editor, scriptwriter, journalist, short-story writer, and novelist, she was one of the best-known writers of the early part of the twentieth century. Along the way, she served as correspondent and columnist for *Christian Herald,* as well as writing books such as *Cross Roads* (1919), *The Island of Faith* (1921), *The Stars Come Close* (1936), and *Singing on the Road* (1936).

Joseph Leininger Wheeler

CITY OF DREAMS

A train pulled out of Washington's Union Station. Among the hundreds of passengers were a man and a woman. But not together. Not together in any way.

*H*e was *not* in a good mood. For one thing, an accident on the Beltway backed traffic up for miles—he almost missed the train. For good measure, outside newly glorified and resurrected Union Station, the trees stood naked, shivering leafless in the biting December wind; the snow was grungy and mud-spattered; the sky was a stolid, unresponsive slate gray; and as if all that weren't enough, the acid icing on the cake was that terrible newspaper headline screaming at him from the newsstands.

He dashed from the parking lot to the station, ran through the station, and at last reached the porter of the Chicago car just as he was preparing to board and close the door. He smoothed his dark, wind-tossed hair back into place and drew a hand across his rugged features, as if by so doing he could blot out the past few days. Oblivious to the glances that followed his tall, lean, and well-dressed figure, he strode down the aisle, looking for a seat. The train jolted into motion. With a sigh of relief he sank into a window seat, thankful he had no seatmate.

Slowly at first, then with gradually increasing speed, the train clackety-clacked its way through back corridors of the nation's capital (unlovely too) as the December sun withdrew west of the Blue Ridge.

Night fell.

The man at the window looked out at a vast sea of lights, but saw only a luminescent blur, heard nothing but the repetitive hum of steel wheels on steel rails and the mournful blasts of the air horn. When he'd collapsed into his seat shortly before, he'd been nothing more than a contorted bundle of shrieking nerves, so tightly

wound that one little half turn more would have shattered his mainspring. Never in his life had he been this
close to that ultimate darkness. His heart pounded
wildly, completely out of control.

Several hours passed before he came back to reality.
The only image he could bring partly into focus in his
foggy mind was that of the porter checking his ticket
some time before, and even that was shrouded in mist.
Suddenly he could hear people talking, could hear a boy
and girl quarreling over a toy, could hear a baby cry. He
was not alone after all.

Tension so filled him that he did not walk down to
the dining car for something to eat. Instead he asked
directions to the observation car; when he puffed to the
top of the stairs, he felt as though he had dragged half of
Washington behind him. Three seats from the front, he
found an unclaimed window.

Of course it would have been quicker to fly, but he
needed—desperately needed—time to think, to hide,
before he faced those he knew again.

At long last, the accumulated tensions began to leave
him, much like a slow leak in an automobile tire.
Kaleidoscopic images and sounds came and went in
seeming incoherence: low bridges and overpasses with
their green, yellow, and red signals, Christmas lights in
city streets, endless caravans of twin-eyed cars, trucks
lit up like Coney Island, signals at crossings, sirens of
ambulances and police cars, the now friendly clackety-
clack, and the soothing echo of what reminded him of
a foghorn. That horn sound was the last sound he
could remember as his body, battered almost beyond

belief, shut down its engines and coasted through the night.

It was early morning before awareness slowly came back to him. Though the train had stopped a number of times during the night, he had been aware of none of them. Now, as the train gained speed on the west-ward slope of the Alleghenies and dawn began to break through the mountain mists, he changed position, burrowed deeper into the warm log-cabin quilt made for him by his mother seven Christmases ago, and went back to sleep.

An intercom call to breakfast woke him up at last. Brushing the cobwebs out of his eyes, he looked down at his wrist as his gold and platinum watch gradually came into focus. It was 8:47 and broad—almost glaringly bright—daylight. Suddenly, he was ravenously hungry.

After freshening up with a shave and a change of clothes, he stashed his belongings and found his way to the dining car. White tablecloths, gold-edged china, and iridescent goblets pleased his eyes. He was seated at a table with a retired couple from Edinburgh, Scotland, and a shoe salesman from Atlanta. Words were sparse because no one took the lead.

Halfway through his Spanish omelette, an attractive young woman in her early-to-mid-thirties followed a waiter to a table at the other end of the car. He caught only a glimpse of her face but did take in the small feet, well-turned legs, and slim figure, inhaling the faintest scent of expensive French perfume as she walked down the swaying aisle and was seated with her back to him.

Then it was back to the observation car. They had traded wooded west Pennsylvania for the snow-covered farmlands of Ohio. Here the snow, blinding white, made the world seem pristine, untouched by civilization's heavy hand. It was only now and here, as he and the small city of travelers floated ever westward, that he faced himself in the tribunal of his mind. Here on this train where no one knew him, he realized with a jolt just how small was his inside-the-Beltway fame. The warm and loving family seated just behind him reminded him of how much he missed having children of his own; the ever-so-much-in-love couple three seats ahead brought home to him how unutterably lonely he was without a soul mate.

Inexorably, though he fought him every step of the way, the bailiff of his mind forced him back to those Washington headlines of yesterday—could it have been only yesterday? He had been his friend, the senator had, as good a friend as he had known for a long time. No senator had been more revered than he—or more *loved*. Always the champion of the underdog, a rock of integrity in a sleazy age, he had become over the years almost a folk icon. Lately, there had been talk of his running for president; the nation seemingly yearned for another Lincoln.

And then came that snowy morning he wished with every fiber of his being that he could forget. When he got to the network building late that morning—massive backup on the Beltway—, he found a note on his office chair from his boss; it was short and terrifying:

Charles,
  Come to my office just as soon as you get in.
  We need to talk.
  J. R.

All the way down the hall, all the way up to the top floor, he wondered what it was that he had done wrong. Was he to get the axe like Henry had last week? Completely out of the blue; just as it had been with Susan two days before. The entire staff was near paranoid about the station's long slip in the ratings. Rumor had it that heads were going to roll, from top to bottom. Since the hostile takeover of the new owners, no one's job was safe for there was no corporate memory at the top. And if he were next? *What would I do? I am overextended on three credit cards; I shouldn't really have purchased that Lexus last July; nor should I have borrowed to take that last cruise. If I'm fired, where could I go? How could I face all those who tell me I'm next in line for the big time?*

He walked into the impressive reception area of the chief, which seemed expressly designed to awe subordinates into submission. He waited a long time—close to an hour. Meanwhile, he died inside. Finally he got the nod to enter. That walk to the other end of the room was one of the longest he could remember. The chief did not smile but merely looked at him—silently—for what seemed like forever with his cold, fishy eyes.

Then he told him. Reminded him that the ratings were bad and getting worse, deep personnel cuts were imminent. Unless the rating decline was reversed, the station might not survive at all. What they needed was a

miracle. Then he smiled for the first time, an *evil* smile.
The miracle had been found: a story had surfaced—
never mind from where—about a prominent senator,
one of the uncrowned kings of the Hill. It had to do
with something the senator had done many years ago
when he was young. Just between the two of them, the
documentation was shaky, the source unreliable (had
perjured himself more than once), but the bottom line
was this: *We need the story. True or not!*

Yes, it concerned his friend the senator, the one who
had done him many good turns over the years, had been
his mentor, in fact. Had welcomed him as a son into his
family. And now here was his chief telling him that this
was his one and only chance; if he refused to break the
story under his own name, and stand behind it, he could
clean out his desk; a severance check would be mailed
to him later. Given no time to deliberate and pressed for
an immediate answer, he caved in. Next day the story
hit Washington and the nation like a 8.5 earthquake,
and he was treated as a celebrity. The chief praised him
and raised his salary 50 percent. Without bothering to
ascertain whether or not the story was true, the harpies
of the media went into a feeding frenzy, the speculation
and innuendo going far beyond the original accusation.
Declaring the senator through—was the nicest thing
they said about him.

And yesterday morning the senator had been felled by
a massive stroke—instantly fatal.

Now, the morning after, Charles stood face-to-face
with his conscience. He was reminded of the Huey
Long prototype in Robert Penn Warren's *All the King's
Men,* who maintained that, if one only searched long

enough and hard enough, sooner or later in the strata of the years, no matter how good the person, *something* could be found with which he could be destroyed. So it had come to pass, with this one not-so-small qualifier: Charles strongly doubted that the story was true.

Now burning thoughts rushed at him, searing his heart and soul with sizzling tears: It is said that there is no such thing as a true friend in Rome on the Potomac; not one of those supposed friends wouldn't stab you in the back if the stakes were high enough. Same for the media. With 500 cable channels needing to be fed, their collective maw is insatiable and not very picky about whether a story be true or not, so long as it is sensational and can help ratings. . . . And here I am, one of the worst! A Judas to my best friend in Washington.

Is this the life I wish to live? A life devoid of friendship, kindness, respect, integrity, empathy—or even simple goodness? Is this what I want my life to represent when I am gone: that I never passed up an opportunity to tear down rather than build up?

His self-recriminations skidded to a halt as the woman of the dining car walked past him to the front seat; as she turned to sit down, for the first time he had the opportunity to study her face. To begin with, it was not one a red-blooded male was likely to forget; furthermore, it bore undeniable signs of trouble: her lovely brows were wrinkled with inner concerns, and her eyes met no one's—like himself, she was traveling in a self-contained world.

Beautiful women were nothing new to him: through the years, a number of them had come into his life; and

all of them had gone on. Some of them might have
stayed had he but asked them to, but he hadn't; for he
had long ago developed a horror of commitment. Like
Oscar Wilde's Dorian Gray, he lived only for today—
and for his ego. But now he felt his body clock ticking:
this Christmas Eve he would be forty. FORTY.
FORTY! Life was passing him by.

A white country church with its sky-seeking steeple
outside his window reminded him of a subject he rarely
thought much about anymore: God. When he spoke
about spiritual things, invariably it was in jest, in ridi-
cule. But that church reminded him of his childhood; to
just such a church had his parents brought him every
Sabbath. He had once believed, and God had once been
central in his life—but all that was before . . . before . . .
even after all the long years he could not face thinking
about it without a catch in the throat, without tears. All
that was before his father had left his mother, brother,
and himself for another woman. From that day to this
he had refused to set foot inside a church (other than for
an occasional concert or funeral). But now, with yesterday's headlines still torching within, he was no longer so
sure about his way of life. In fact, he felt bankrupt of all
the positive qualities the senator had embodied prior to
the day Charles helped destroy him. The senator had
often invited him to attend church with him; every
time, he had declined. And the senator's wife had been
like a mother to him. His own mother had died just
two years ago: had skidded through a guardrail on
Highway 1 during a spring storm. Her passing left a
great empty space in his soul; great guilt, too, for she
had prayed for him every day, prayed that he would

invite God back into his life—he never had. At the
remembering service they had for her, he had kept his
composure until the last—until someone had sung
Mother's favorite song, "Tenderly He Watches over
You." Then he broke down and cried until there were
no more tears to cry.

Indiana swept by, but he didn't see it. Then came Illinois, and the skyscrapers of Chicago could be seen.
Everyone was called back to their seats. The train shud-
dered to a stop, and the city within a city disembarked.

During the six-hour wait, Charles walked the streets
near the train station. He walked because he didn't want
to face the headlines—the same subject regardless of the
newspaper. One headline really jolted him: the column,
written by a respected journalist, questioned the veracity
of his now famous "scoop." It seemed as though, thread
by thread, the fabric of his life was unraveling, and he
did not know where there might be a stopping place.

On one of these streets, the front door of a century-
old cathedral stood open; for some inexplicable reason,
Charles felt impelled to go in. An organist—renowned,
it turned out—was interpreting Bach. The very floor
shook. Charles found a seat in a dark corner and let the
music bombard his soul. Wave after wave thundered in
and engulfed him. During "Jesu, Joy of Man's Desiring,"
he chanced to look up at a stained glass window depicting
Christ with the one lost sheep. Without knowing how he
got there, Charles found himself on his knees, shedding
the first tears since his mother's death. What all this
meant, he did not know. All he knew was that, in some
unexplainable way, he had turned a corner. His last words

before he stood to his feet were, "Lord, guide me, please—bring someone to show me the way."

He almost missed this train, too! He had lost all track of time in the cathedral, having it out with his soul. The train was already moving, in fact, but the porter in the last car, seeing him sprinting along the track, helped him swing aboard. Just in time he had remembered his suitcases in two terminal lockers. Relieved not to be left behind, he moved up through the cars of the City of Dreams until he came to the two set aside for through passengers to Portland. As he entered his car, halfway down on the right, the sun chose that moment to shine through between buildings on a now familiar figure, a woman by the window, a woman with rich brown hair, burnished with copper. She turned to smile at a three-year-old child across the aisle, and her smile was both tender and yearning. It stopped him in his tracks. As quickly as it had come, it was gone, and she had turned back to the window. She was alone, and she wasn't a woman one expected to find alone. He found his heart pounding as he neared her seat, and to his chagrin, his broadcast-quality voice shook a little when he asked her if the aisle seat was taken. She said no graciously and picked up a book on that seat so he could sit down. Then she resumed her viewing out the window. But she had to look his way when the porter came to check their tickets: Both were checked through to western Oregon, so then he realized, to his inner delight, that they'd be traveling together for almost three days. Much could happen in that length of time. Charles was amazed at himself, for he was known in the D.C. area as one of the most effective and persistent television interviewers around. He had worked his way up the ladder, each rung solid below his feet before he moved to the next. In recent months and years, more and more important assignments had come his way. More than a mere photogenic talking head, his encyclopedic knowledge of people, history, geography, and the political process gave him a distinct edge; a razor-edged wit and a disarming ability to laugh at himself did the rest. He'd been told the anchor job was as good as his sometime the next spring. He had enjoyed being important, being on a first-name basis with the nation's power brokers. There was no one he dared not tackle one-on-one in a hard-hitting interview. Yet here he sat next to about 120 pounds of feminine beauty, and he found himself unable to get a conversation going. Where was his vaunted glibness now?

She opened her book and began reading. Kibitzing a bit, he discovered that it bore the title of *Quo Vadis;* he had heard about the book years before but knew virtually nothing about it. Suddenly he found himself discomfited: He didn't even know what to do with his hands. He got up, and out of his suitcase in the overhead rack he pulled out the latest issue of *Newsweek.* Mindlessly, he leafed through it, back to front, not knowing at all what was on any given page; suddenly, at the front of the magazine, he discovered that the lead article had to do with his "friend," the senator, and his perceived chances for the presidency. He froze there, the magazine open, and the kindly face of the senator staring at him with the well-known chuckle lines in his face and the impish twinkle Charles had come to love. The woman at the window chanced to look at the image and broke the silence. "Oh! did you see the papers today? Wasn't that terrible news about the senator! . . . Almost tears my heart out, for he was one of the good guys, one of the only political figures in Washington I really respected. . . . What a president he would have made! And now, just like that, he's gone!" And, with a catch in her throat, she turned back to the window. Charles found his face turning crimson, unable to say a word. He wondered if she knew who had broken the story. Oh, how he hoped not!

The City of Dreams finally shook itself free of Chicago and its multitudinous suburbs, and with ever increasing speed turned west. The woman at the window read on, engrossed in her book—he still didn't know her name. Ostensibly he was reading the latest Grisham novel he'd retrieved from his suitcase, but in reality not a word was registering in his mind, for he saw but her, drank in but her, and inhaled but the ever-so-faint fragrance of her.

Once she looked up, and he dared to say, "Must be quite a book!" and she smiled as she looked down again, saying simply, "*That* it is!" and resumed reading. Stymied there, he tried to resume *his* reading but couldn't, for the print continued to blur and the words made no sense at all. He thought of going to the observation car but was riveted to his chair, not wanting to lose a millisecond of the vision at the window. It wasn't just her looks or her perfect form that took his breath away—it was something far deeper. In her hazel eyes were mirrored sorrow, pain, and heartbreak, but also strength, courage, and joy. He only sensed these things, for he had looked straight into her eyes only a couple of

times; but as an interviewer he had learned years ago
that the eyes are indeed the window to the soul: they
alone cannot lie. What he *did* know was this: One could
look into those eyes for a lifetime and never plumb their
depths. Never before had he been in close quarters with
eyes like these.

In December, evening comes early, so soon the
curtains of night descended on the prairies. There was
no sunset because a snowstorm was sweeping down out
of Alberta—a "Canadian clipper" the engineer called it.
At first the flakes floated lazily down, but that changed
quickly as the full force of the storm was felt. Not much
could be seen, except through the lights of small towns
they passed through, but the wind could certainly be felt
and heard.

Around eight o'clock Charles asked his seatmate if she
was hungry; she was, so they found their way down the
swaying train to the dining car. They were seated across
from a young couple—honeymooning, it turned out—
from Bavaria. Their destination was Monument Valley
and the Grand Canyon, two places they had long
dreamed of seeing. In the process of introducing themselves, Charles finally learned the name of the woman
at the window—it was Michelle. The German couple,
Hans and Hildie, had been waiting all day for the
opportunity to ask somebody questions about the West,
so both Charles and Michelle lost their shyness quickly
as they assumed the thrust-upon-them roles of host and
hostess. How Michelle sparkled and dimpled as she
helped to answer the many questions. And of course
she and Charles had questions, too, about the Bavarian

Alps, especially about the fairytale castles of Mad King Ludwig. Since it was Hildie's birthday, a waiter brought them a candlelit cake—which eventually led to questions as to their birth dates.

By the time they walked back to their seats they were friends; now he was eager to learn more about her. He learned that she was the daughter of a small-town minister, had been educated at a midwestern Bible college, double majoring in speech and journalism, subsequently completing the course work for the master's in philosophy and a Ph.D. in theology at Vanderbilt; she was just now beginning on her dissertation—subject: the early Christians during the time of the Emperor Nero—that's why she was so fascinated with Sienkiewicz's *Quo Vadis*. She currently worked as an assistant editor of a newspaper on Maryland's eastern shore and was heading home to Astoria, adjacent to Oregon's northwesternmost cape.

How about him? Well, he was a child of divorce, educated at St. Johns in Annapolis, master's in history at University of Maryland in College Park, and Ph.D. in history of ideas at Georgetown. Worked now for a Beltway TV station and was planning on spending Christmas with his only brother and family, who lived near Timberline Lodge on Mt. Hood. He did not then tell her that he hadn't seen his brother in twenty-one years and that his brother was dying from a rare disease for which there was no known cure. It was clear that her family was warm, loving, close, and Christian—and his was all that hers was not.

About an hour or so later, he asked her about *Quo Vadis*. Would she mind telling him what it was about?

She was silent a moment or two, then, choosing her words carefully, said, "Well, it's about a princess from ancient Poland named Lygia and a Roman tribune named Vinitius. She is secretly a member of the early Christian church and he does not believe in religion at all—I don't want to give away the plot, but the story has to do with Nero, the burning of Rome, and the terrible persecution of the early Christians."

"And Lygia and Vin—Vin—uh . . ."

"Vinitius."

"Oh yes, Vinitius . . . what happens to them?"

Even in the darkness he could sense her smile: "For *that,* you'll just have to read the book yourself."

Not long afterward, Michelle wrapped a light train blanket around her shoulders, positioned a small pillow against the window, and dropped off to sleep. But for Charles, sleep did not come that easily. Thoughts swirled around in his head like a Tornado Alley twister. There was so much to think about that he felt incapable of sorting it out. Every minute that passed, the City of Dreams carried him farther away from the nightmare he had left behind in Washington; in some respects, he felt himself to be in a different world, a time warp—a world he was increasingly reluctant to ever leave.

His thoughts brought him to that slender form leaning against the window, sleeping naturally and easily as only those with a clear conscience can. He knew very little about her, for she was adept at erecting barriers between small talk and personal talk. Obviously she had had a lot of practice dealing with men like him down through the years. Well he knew that many, if not most, of the human moths that flutter around the flame of beauty are there for no good. For her own self-preservation, a beauty must develop a thick veneer; at that, most beauties have disastrous marriages. Almost invariably, they are sought out and courted for all the wrong reasons. Certainly his track record in this respect had been no different. He sighed.

The midnight hours passed and the sleeping form remained only a touch away—but he found himself responding to her unspoken trust in him. Gradually there was stealing over him something totally new in his adult lifetime—tenderness. So new, in fact, that at first he did not even recognize what it was. About 2:00 A.M., the train stopped in a small prairie town. Christmas lights could be seen inside house windows and outside on eaves and trees. Now he could see, through the light from street lamps, just how thick and fast the snow was coming down. Half an hour passed, an hour, and the car gradually became colder. When Michelle had twice shivered in her dreams, he quietly stood up, retrieved the warm log-cabin quilt, leaned over and, ever so gently, wrapped it around her. A deep sigh told him that her subconscious had gratefully acknowledged the difference. People around them began to awaken and question each other. Finally a steward came through the car, explaining the situation in whispers to those who stopped him: The problem had to do with a connecting train slowed by near-blizzard conditions to the north. So many passengers were transferring to this train that it was felt they just *had* to wait.

A little over two hours after the train stopped, the other train loomed ghostlike out of the darkness and falling snow. Soon the sounds of doors opening, footsteps, people bumping into things, directions from stewards, questioning whines from sleepy children, and fretful babies, added to blasts of frigid air from the open doors below, woke up most of those still sleeping—finally, even Michelle. Initially, she seemed disoriented, not knowing at all where she was; gradually, awareness came back to her, and last of all, she began to question how that blessedly warm quilt had come to her.

She turned to him, smiled a sleepy smile, and said, "Out with it: How did I acquire this quilt? And furthermore, what in the world's happening? It's *cold* in here!" So he told her all that had transpired. She looked at him with softened eyes.

"You wrapped me with your mother's quilt so I wouldn't get cold, yet there you sit shivering! Come, Charles, this is a big quilt—got to be at least a queen!—here, take this end of it and get warm!" Implicit in her words was this: *What a man this is! Not only did he not make passes in the dark, but he covered me so I'd be warm, remaining icy cold himself. Now I know he can be trusted.*

Suddenly there was a jerk, then another, and the now full train was on its way again. Everyone—especially those on the late train who had been worrying they'd be left in a cold train station for another day—quickly dropped off to sleep, Michelle almost instantly, Charles about an hour later. A couple of times during the night he heard the muted sound of the air horn far in front, but it was a good sound, a comforting sound, and he smiled listening to it.

Morning came at last, and the City of Dreams hurtled through time and space, trying to make up for the lost time. Stiffly, yet quietly, Charles stood up, so as to not awaken the sleeping woman at the window, then went downstairs for his shave, ablutions, and change of clothes. As he climbed the stairs, the train began slowing down, for the Queen City of the Plains, Denver, was just ahead. The snow continued to fall, but more lightly now. When he got back to his seat, Michelle had just awakened, and sat gazing at him through adorably sleepy eyes. He could hardly control his runaway heart.

She excused herself and returned twenty minutes later with her cheeks a freshly scrubbed pink and her shiny hair pulled into a loose knot. A short polar fleeced shirt floated over the soft cotton mock turtleneck tucked into stonewashed jeans. She seemed as comfortable in this Rocky Mountain naturalist look as she had in the tailored silk blouse, wool jacket, skirt, and dress boots she had worn onto the train the first day.

At Denver, they disembarked, ordered breakfast in a nearby café, reboarded, and the Amtrak City of Dreams began the long, long climb to Moffat Tunnel. As they climbed, the volume of snow increased as well. Once through the tunnel, they found seats in the observation car, knowing that the scenery from there on was about as beautiful and spectacular as can be seen from a train track in America. Frozen rivers, ice-edged waterfalls, snow-flocked trees; Winter Park, Fraser, Gore Canyon, Glenwood Canyon, and still the snow continued to fall, but intermittently now. Here and there they saw elk, deer, bald eagles, and once a snow-encrusted fox that watched them go by with quizzical eyes.

Then came night once again, and they moved back to their car. Both found themselves strangely shy and quiet during dinner. Once their hands touched, reaching for bread, and an electric shock passed through his arm. They didn't talk much afterward; both were tired, but especially *him,* for the stress of the last few days had begun to wear him down. This time it was he who fell asleep first, and this time it was she who watched him, watched and wondered.

When they woke up, outside their window was the Salt Lake City train station. The snow had stopped during the night, and the morning was golden. Oh, it was a heart-stoppingly beautiful day! They disembarked and walked joyously through the newly fallen snow, so dazzling and white. This morning, there was a different look in her eyes when she looked at him, yet almost nothing personal had been discussed in their conversations together. Then the "all aboard" signal was given, and the long silver snake headed north to Idaho.

Both seemed aware that, unless a miracle occurred, this would be the last full day they would ever spend together, but nothing was said about it—not until they had come back from the dining car in early afternoon. Deep within him, Charles knew with absolute certainty that he loved her already as he had never loved another in his almost forty years of selfish life. She awakened in him a yearning for real friendship-based companionship. Oh, the fires of desire burned within him at the sight of her, but they were now tempered by tenderness, concern for her comfort and well-being. And a fierce but gentle protectiveness. Should he lose her, he felt confident that he would never find another who could compare to her, so in truth it was now or never.

But he also knew that he was at the turning point of his life in other respects: career-wise, for starters; relationship with friends and family; and, more importantly, his new post-cathedral experience with God. In those respects, Michelle could not have entered his life at a worse time. Yet, had he not been at these crossroads, would he even be thinking this way about her? He couldn't help but notice that she bowed her head and prayed before each meal, so clearly, that relationship had priority over all others in her life.

Suddenly a little boy stood beside him, the just-turned-five-year-old perpetual motion machine who belonged to the family six rows behind him. Children had full run of the train—to them it was one long playground. The child—Tony—was *always* asking questions. Earlier that morning Charles had heard the boy's mother plaintively saying to a woman across the aisle, "Yes, Tony is the youngest of four—had he been the oldest, he'd have been an only child." Big Tony, Tony's father, had quite a story to tell. He and his twin brother had been adopted out to separate parents, shortly after birth; neither ever knew what happened to the other. But, in recent years, Tony had instituted a search for that brother who represented such a large missing piece of his self-hood. Now, thirty-six years later, that brother had been found—and Big Tony and family were to spend Christmas with them. Thanks to Little Tony, everyone in their car now knew the story. Well, here was Little Tony staring at him and Michelle, engrossed again in *Quo Vadis*. In his high, piping voice, which the entire car could hear perfectly, he asked a question that had been troubling him: "Are you two in love?"

Charles just sat there in a state of shock; by the window a lovely brunette was blushing seven shades of scarlet. All Charles could think of to say was "Why do you ask?" In the vicinity of the boy's father came an embarrassed "Tony! What a rude question to ask!"

But Tony didn't consider it rude. So he answered, "Sometimes you act like you're in love—the way you sort of look at each other when the other isn't looking. If you're not, it sorta' seems like you'd like to be."

Then he was gone, forcibly retrieved by the strong arms of his father. But the little rascal got in the last word after all: As Big Tony propelled his unquenchable heir back to the bosom of his what-can-he-possibly-say-or-do-next family, the familiar voice piped up once more, loud and clear, "But Daddy, questions help me know things!" Waves of laughter rolled through the car. Michelle found something unusually interesting to look at outside her window.

When his heartbeat had returned to normal, Charles thought again about Big Tony and the missing piece of his life waiting for him in eastern Oregon—just as *his* brother, a missing piece too, was waiting for him. A portion of his family who might not be around much longer. How foolish to have wasted all these years! Why hadn't he bridged the abyss between them sooner?

He was reminded that time was fast running out on another front—and that realization decided him.

Turning to the woman at the window, in a voice that shook in spite of his determination to keep it steady, he said, "Michelle, when you come to a good stopping point, I'd like very much to share something with you."

With a smile, she slid her marker in and closed the book, then said, "No better time than now—what is it?"

He said, "It'll take a while, Michelle, but I have a very special reason for wanting to tell you a story."

"Y-e-e-s?" she asked, somewhat uncertainly.

So, greatly condensed, he told her the story of his life, told it truthfully, even though doing so flooded his heart with wave after wave of pain. The Washington years were the hardest of all: When he got to the events of the last week, his pace slowed. He came to a complete halt several times and had to wipe his eyes with his handkerchief. In the telling, he spared not himself, did nothing to minimize the monstrous thing he had done. But he didn't stop there: He told of his first night's torment in the observation car, seeing her and noting the pain lines in her face; and the cathedral, organ, and stained glass window in Chicago.

Then he finished his story with these words:

"If you were just any woman, I wouldn't be telling you this. But you aren't. You have come into my life at a moment when I am all at sea, with many more questions than I have answers, and I am strongly questioning all the values by which I have lived. I wish I could come to you strong, with solutions rather than questions. I did find the biggest solution of all in the cathedral, though. First and foremost, I now know that a life without God just isn't worth living; the same is true of values based on biblical principles. I didn't even know whether God would accept me back, but I prayed in Chicago that He would forgive the Prodigal Son that was me—and He did. I asked Him to send me someone to guide my stumbling steps; I know so little about how to get right with God.

"Second, I feel the time has come for a major career change—I can no longer work for a boss I cannot respect—even loathe—but I haven't the slightest idea where I'll go from there—I only know I cannot work there another day.

"Third, even though it will be the hardest thing I have done in my lifetime, I shall never live at peace with myself until I ask the senator's wife for forgiveness, for the despicable thing I did to her husband.

"Fourth, I plan to make family central in my life: to love and cherish my brother, and show it; and should I lose him, to serve as a surrogate father to his family.

"Fifth, and I know full well what a risk I am taking in even saying this, but it is a greater risk *not* to. Some people don't believe in love at first sight—I know I never did—but I do now. From the first moment I saw you, my heart yearned toward you, and I loved you without even knowing you. During the last couple of days I have only come to love you more, even without hearing your story. Believe me, I know how sudden this must seem to you, but I am not asking for a response. Even if you should say, 'Charles, you have more gall than I have ever known, and I want nothing more to do with you—ever!' Even if that be true, I plead for but one favor: Do me the kindness of telling me your own story."

She did not meet his eyes but stared out the window, absolutely silent, for what seemed like forever to him. He could only wait by her side, leaving his fate in her hands. Finally, she turned from the window, stared straight ahead for a few pensive moments, then began to speak, but refusing to meet his eyes:

"I was born to a man and a woman who deeply loved each other—they still do." Then she went on to tell him *her* unvarnished story: The brief period of rebellion against her parents; the times when she questioned God; the career problems she had faced, and was still facing; and the story of Richard. They had fallen in love at the midwestern Bible college, he had asked her to marry him, and she had accepted with joy. But, the weekend before the wedding she had found out that he was not the kind of man she could respect, and she most certainly refused to marry a man she could not look up to and admire. So she had called it off—the hardest thing she had ever done, but in retrospect it proved to be the right thing, for he had broken the heart and shattered the life of the girl he ended up marrying several years later. . . . Yes, there had been other opportunities to marry, but in every case, love and respect never coalesced in any one man—"Guess I've been too picky, but I've determined that not until I find a man who loves me as much as my father loves my mother, who I can respect as much as I respect my father, and who I can love as much as my mother loves my father—only then shall I marry.

"Lately everything seems empty. Men seem to see no deeper than my outward appearance. I want them to see my caring heart. And I've always known that marriage between a believer and a nonbeliever would not work, bringing with it a lifetime of sorrow and misunderstandings; as for the children, almost invariably they'd be lost to the Lord, unless a miracle occurred.

"My deepest crisis hit when I held the newborn child of a dear friend. I've always yearned for God's greatest gift—children—but the dull ache increased to life-shattering pain when I held that baby! My biological clock didn't just tick, it exploded! All the suppressed longing for a home, a soul mate, for children, burst open inside me just the day before I boarded this train. The pain you saw in my eyes reflected my anguished pleading with God to end my long years of loneliness— if that be His will."

Then she was silent again, looking out the window for a long time. Idly, she picked up *Quo Vadis,* but kept losing her place, a far-off look in her eyes. But at no time did she establish eye contact with him.

Night came, and they were as they had been at the beginning: casual strangers churning out small talk. It was as though each had raised the shade to enable the other to see the naked soul, then after doing so, lowered it again, and then gone on as though the shades had never been raised. It was almost surreal.

Dinner was quiet, and Michelle was absent-minded; Charles was just plain miserable. Had he been stupid to be that candid with her? But how could he *not* have been?

But afterward, remembering what he had said to her about praying for a guide, she spoke to him about God, assured him that of course God had accepted him; it was never too late to come back, as long as life pulsed in his veins. They talked far into the night, about things that since childhood had held no interest for him—God, the plan of salvation, and how God seeks wandering children and brings them home again. He asked questions far into the night, and she answered them all. Shortly after midnight, he gave his heart to the Lord, and she took his hand as she prayed a prayer of dedication, and he followed with a prayer of commitment.

He was long in going to sleep, filled as he was with both a feeling of great joy and great loss. He could see that he had gained the Lord. But gaining her was not to be. Finally, he fell into a restless sleep.

They were descending the corkscrew Blue Mountains when the first rays of Christmas Eve Day came through the window. Michelle woke first. She looked across at Charles, his face drawn and etched with pain, yet at the same time illuminated by a joy and peace that had not been there before. She stepped over his legs without awakening him and found her way into the observation car—to think, and to pray.

Some time later, she returned to her car just as the train was slowing to its first top in the Columbia River gorge. An air of excitement filled the car. This was it: the thirty-six-year moment of truth. She stopped in the vestibule as Big Tony and family, carrying gaily colored packages and suitcases, got off the train into the cold, foggy morning. But there, to greet them, it seemed, must have been the entire town, complete with banners, band, and balloons—and the other brother. She watched as the two brothers dropped everything, like two gunless gunmen in *High Noon*—then ran to each other. That entire side of the train cheered!

Then she glanced at Charles, expecting to see on his face a reflection of Tony's joy. Instead, she found him leaning against the window, his shoulders shaking with gut-wrenching sobs. *It's his brother,* she thought. *No wonder he had a hard time finally telling me about him!* At that moment, a dam deep within her broke, sweeping with it the wreckage and anguish of the long, lonely years. She knew full well he was a deeply flawed man, yet who but God could be perfect? His Christian walk was a new one rather than one strengthened by time; there, she would have to lead, at least at first. Should she accept him, there would be a tough road ahead—job-wise and financially—for both of them, for she, too, had tired of the artificiality of her life, the six million people she could never get away from in the Washington-Baltimore corridor, and the simple life and faith she missed.

And she longed for the ever-changing mighty breakers of the Pacific with every atom of her being. Her uncle owned a newspaper in Astoria, and it needed both a publisher and editor; his last letter had urged her to take one of those positions and find someone for the other, as he was old, ill, and tired. Perhaps that would be the answer (Charles too had told her how he was tired of urban life and wanted to live near the sea). Astoria would be a good place to raise children—neither of them were too old for parenthood *yet.*

Again her eyes took in the Christmas celebration outside her window—the coming home of two lost boy-men, the engulfing, the smiling through tears. In her heart, Tony was Charles, also going home to a brother after the long years. Suddenly, the last inner barrier was swept away—can one ever really know another? She hadn't really known Richard—and they had dated for four years. Even after a lifetime together, a man and woman still wear masks before each other. No, time is not always the answer. In a sudden flash of clarity she realized that it isn't length of association that roots love, but the sharing of ideals, hopes, dreams—God. Two can grow together.

The only questions remaining were these: Did she respect that man by the window as much as she did her father? No . . . not yet—that was a mighty tall order— but quite likely would in time. Could she grow to love that man by the window as her mother loved her father? Could she? Of *course* she could! To get off the City of Dreams without him would be, would be . . . she couldn't even visualize it, it would hurt too much. Now she knew that true love rarely makes sense: it is either there or it isn't. It's a realization that life without each other is not even an option. Even when heaven and hell come together within it, even should it last but a day, an hour, that moment shared would be worth it all. All at once she realized that, unbeknownst to her, the Lord had answered her prayer, had brought to her a man, a man who would give her love and tenderness, friend-ship and understanding, wrapped up in protectiveness, and tied with strength—oh, what greater Christmas gift could a woman ever ask for than *this!*

The City of Dreams jolted once more into motion, a blizzard of hands waving from both sides of the windows. The City of Dreams was, after all, just that—

every last man, woman, and child had first boarded the train with dreams, dreams that they hoped would be fulfilled when they reached the other end. So, it was not mere advertising hype to call it "City of Dreams."

Beyond the city limits and heading down the great river to Portland, Charles turned to find her in his old seat, glory in her eyes.

At first, he could not even fathom the change in her: the new tenderness in her eyes, the new so-much-more in her eyes, the new *everything!* His eyes widened.

Then her made-to-be-kissed lips curved adorably, lips he had yet to touch. She shattered his composure first, with what day it was: "Happy Birthday, Charlie."

Then she completed the demolition with, "Merry Christmas, Darling."